## Zach caught Pilar watching him with a strange expression. Was it wariness?

She looked away, but Zach continued to study her. She was dressed in what he would describe as one of her trademark outfits: a ruffled, feminine blouse and a pair of black slacks.

Others might have been surprised that he could give such detail about a woman he didn't know well, but as a police detective, it was his job to remember details.

The most notable detail was how natural Pilar appeared, swaying with a baby she'd just discovered, literally, on the doorstep.

TINY BLESSINGS: Giving thanks for the neediest of God's children, and the families who take them in!

\* \* \*

**Books by Dana Corbit**

Love Inspired

## DANA CORBIT

has been fascinated with words since third grade, when she began stringing together stanzas of rhyme. That interest, and an inherent nosiness, led her to a career as a newspaper reporter and editor. After earning state and national recognition in journalism, she traded her career for stay-at-home motherhood.

But the need for creative expression followed her home, and later through the move from Indiana to Milford, Michigan. Outside the office, Dana discovered the joy of writing fiction. In stolen hours, during naps and between carpooling and church activities, she escapes into her private world, telling stories from her heart.

Dana makes her home in Michigan with her husband, three young daughters and two cats.

# ON THE DOORSTEP

## DANA CORBIT

Steeple Hill®

Published by Steeple Hill Books™

To my editor, Diane Dietz, for guarding my "p's" and "q's."
Thank you for your constant support and your willingness to juggle all the details so I can simply tell the stories I love. To my personal "doctor.com," Celia D'Errico, D.O., who helps me to get the medical facts straight. I so appreciate your brilliance and your friendship.
To my sister-in-law, Vivian Berry, for your great Puerto Rican accent and sweet spirit, and to my brother, Todd Berry, for having the good sense to marry such a cool *chica*. And, finally to my POTL gang of critique partners, Nancy Gideon, Laurie Kuna, Loralee Lillibridge, Victoria Schab and Constance Smith, who freely share their time and talent with me.
Though we are miles apart, I carry all of you, my friends, in my heart.

Special thanks and acknowledgment are given to Dana Corbit for her contribution to the TINY BLESSINGS series.

**STEEPLE HILL BOOKS**

Steeple
Hill®

ISBN 0-373-87326-3

ON THE DOORSTEP

Copyright © 2005 by Steeple Hill Books, Freiburg Switzerland

www.SteepleHill.com

**Printed in U.S.A.**

By this all men will know that you are
My disciples, if you have love for one another.
—*John* 13:35

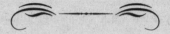

Zach—A Hebrew name meaning "God remembers, remembrance of the Lord." It is derived from the name Zechariah. There are over thirty men with this name mentioned in the Bible, including the author of the Book of Zechariah.

Pilar—A Spanish name meaning "pillar, support."

Gabriel—Hebrew name meaning "God is my strength." One of seven archangels, Gabriel appeared to Mary to give her the news of her pregnancy and impending birth of Jesus.

# Chapter One

Firsts were supposed to be good things. First loves. First kisses. Scary yet exciting, these beginnings were like birthday presents, wrapped in hope and tied with ribbons of promise. Pilar Estes used to believe all that and more. But as the first of September brought a fuchsia-tinged dawn to Chestnut Grove, Virginia, her morning of premieres only made her feel ashamed.

Last week if her friends had suggested she would dread coming to work, she would have thought they were kidding. It would have seemed impossible. Helping to create families through Tiny Blessings Adoption Agency was her dream job, a fact she'd repeated to anyone who would listen. She'd even earned the duty of starting the office coffeemaker because she was always there first.

This morning she couldn't even gather the energy to get excited about an upcoming child placement. Her eyes filled with tears at just the thought of the office's "Wall of Blessings," the photo collage featuring the agency's many happy adoptive families. If only she could stay home.

That truth humiliated her enough, but it paled by comparison to the shame she felt over her other first that morning. She'd begun to question God's will for her life. Not just small, needling questions, either, but huge, nagging uncertainties with dancing question marks.

Her chest squeezed so tightly that Pilar cracked open her car window so she could gulp in some of the crisp morning breeze. It must have been her imagination that tinged the air with the odor of decay. Labor Day wasn't even until the following Monday, and the leaves didn't usually turn in central Virginia for several more weeks. But her betraying nose, so like her disobedient thoughts, made her wonder if dying dreams had a scent.

What ever happened to "leaning on the everlasting arms," as the old hymn said? She'd always felt so comforted by that hymn and by its reference to Moses' words in the Book of Deuteronomy, "The eternal God is thy refuge, and underneath are the everlasting arms."

Was she one of those people who only trusted when trusting came easy? No, that wasn't true. She'd gone right on believing in God's will during her mother's heart trouble when Pilar was still in college. She'd never stopped praying through Rita Estes's triple-bypass surgery and recovery.

And even at twenty-eight, she'd never questioned

that God, in His time and with His infinite wisdom, would provide her with a home and a family. She'd continued to believe, though she could count her dates the last two years on one hand, and the one man at church she'd seen possibilities in didn't seem to notice her at all.

So why now? Why couldn't she let go of her fears this time instead of being so selfish and secretive with them? Hadn't her psychology degree taught her anything about sharing her problems? Obviously not, because she hadn't mentioned a thing to her parents or to her three best friends, and she'd never kept anything from Meg Talbot Kierney, Rachel Noble and Anne Smith.

Everything might turn out to be fine. Even her gynecologist had said so the day before. She wanted to trust God to take care of the situation; really, she did. She just needed some time to process the news, to accept that she might have more in common with Tiny Blessings' clients than she'd known.

Polycystic ovarian disease. It sounded so complicated, but it was really just a fancy term for a combination of irregular cycles and ovarian cysts that could add up to infertility. Though it was still just a possible diagnosis, to Pilar it felt like a death sentence, at least for the future she's always imagined.

She wouldn't know anything for sure until the ultrasound her doctor had scheduled for Tuesday, but she worked in the adoption business. She understood the prospects. And the possibility hanging heavily over her heart was that even if she found a man to love, there was a chance she could never have his children.

Her nose burned and her vision blurred, but Pilar fought back her tears. She needed to push aside her worries and focus on her job. The coffee wouldn't put itself on, and the Newlins would expect her to be there for their first interview later that morning.

She took a few deep breaths and found some tentative control. Grateful for the comfort of routine, she parked a few buildings past the agency office and backtracked. A gust of wind fluttered her bangs and whipped her long black ponytail over her shoulder. She crossed her arms over her blouse, wishing she'd worn a sweater.

With her gaze on the sidewalk cracks, instead of the narrow former bank building that for thirty-five years had housed Tiny Blessings, she mentally ticked off a list of her other duties before the big Labor Day weekend. A home visit to schedule. An introduction to plan between prospective adoptive parents and a darling toddler with special needs.

"Lord, please help me not to be distracted from my work today," she whispered when her thoughts flitted back to her own needs. Reflexively, she pressed her hand against her lower abdomen, as if she could protect the fragile organs inside. The minor cramps that had brought her into the doctor's office in the first place squeezed again, taunting her.

"Please help me to stay focused," she restated, knowing full well she should have been praying for healing or at least acceptance of God's will.

That she couldn't manage more than that today only frustrated her more. She'd never had patience for weakness in herself, and she wasn't about to go soft now just because she had an upcoming appointment at the hospital.

If she'd been looking up from the sidewalk, she might have seen it sooner, but Pilar was already halfway up the walk before she noticed what looked like a giant lidded picnic basket resting on the building's wide porch.

She jerked to a stop. Images of ticking explosives and chemical contaminants fluttered in her mind's eye, before her good sense returned. She'd been watching too many television action shows. This was Chestnut Grove, she had to remember. Until a few months ago, she could have referred to her city as a real-life Mayberry, until her own agency's horrible discovery of falsified birth records. That was inexcusable. Still, bombs and other big-city mayhem hadn't taken the bus out to Richmond's suburbs yet.

To be safe, Pilar approached the basket slowly, tilting her head and listening for any tick-tick-tick. At first, there was only silence. She snickered. Who did she think she was? Some Sydney Bristow *Alias* wanna-be without the cool disguises and martial arts moves? Her bomb-deactivating skills would probably be wasted on a gift basket from grateful adoptive parents. They occasionally received baskets, though usually during office hours.

Just when she'd gathered the courage to come close and lean over the basket, a strange grunting sound had her jerking her hand back. She listened again and heard the same grunting, *human* sound.

"Oh dear." The words fell from her lips as she lifted the lid. A pair of bright blue eyes stared at her from a little pink face. Pilar didn't move. She couldn't. Seconds must have ticked by, but time stalled in a crystal vacuum as the baby's unblinking gaze and Pilar's frozen stare connected.

Strange how the child wasn't upset, but content, swaddled in a receiving blanket and resting in a nest made of an expensive-looking blanket. But then a louder-pitched grunt splintered the silence as tiny feet kicked against the covering. The perfect round face scrunched and reddened.

"Oh, you poor little thing." Finally able to move again, Pilar dropped her purse and keys and crouched next to the basket. Carefully, she lifted out the baby and loosened the blue receiving blanket that had a race-car pattern. Since the sleeper beneath the blanket was also blue, she assumed the baby was a boy. "How could anyone have left you here like this?"

Her sudden movement and her voice must have startled him because he jerked his hands and kicked his feet. Still, he didn't cry. Warmth spread from the small bundle through Pilar's blouse and into her heart. For several seconds she cradled the child, her body automatically rocking to a silent lullaby.

Pilar drew the side of her thumb down a perfectly formed jaw, the skin satiny beneath her touch. How pale his cheek appeared against her golden skin tone.

Instinctively, the baby turned his head toward the source of stimulation and worked his mouth in search of a meal. Pilar shifted him to her shoulder and stood.

"Sorry, sweetheart. Can't help you with that. But I am going to help you."

Balancing him against her, she crouched for her keys and unlocked the door. She rushed inside, rattled in a way that was so unlike her.

When she reached her desk, she rested her hand on the phone and hesitated. "Call the police and emergency workers first. Then Social Services. Or is it Social Services first?"

Did she really expect the baby to answer? She shook her head, both to answer the ridiculous question and to pull herself together. She could do this. Even if she did work for a private agency rather than Social Services, she still was familiar with laws concerning abandoned children. She'd just never seen one close-up before.

The first newborn wail came as Pilar dialed 911. The pitiful, hungry cry cut straight to her heart, making her feel helpless. She refused to give in to it. Maybe she couldn't meet all of the baby's needs at this moment, but she would do everything she could for him.

Over the noise, she communicated the major details: abandoned live infant, appeared healthy, found at Tiny Blessings Adoption Agency. After she hung up the phone, having been assured that help was on the way, Pilar lowered herself into her office chair.

The baby, though, would have none of it. He continued to protest until Pilar popped back up and started pacing. She walked, she swayed and she rocked. But nothing pacified him until, desperate, she washed her hand and popped her index finger into his mouth. As she moved him into a reclining position, he suckled greedily, still too new to understand he didn't have the real thing.

He was so perfect, a tiny bundle from God that someone didn't have the wisdom to recognize. She would have recognized the gift, would have had the good sense to cherish it.

As she touched his tiny hand, the baby grasped her index finger. Her chest ached. Her eyes filled. It was only another reflex, she reminded herself. He hadn't chosen her and grabbed hold of her. Somehow, though, it still felt as if he had, as if an infant young enough to only differentiate comfort from discomfort had picked her, had placed his future in her hands.

For a blip of a moment, she imagined them as more than foundling and rescuer. In that stolen, secret moment, she was just a regular mother caring for her beautiful son.

In the distance, a siren fractured the silence, bringing her back to the real world where some people abandoned their children, while others only dreamed of a child to hold.

The child dozed in her arms, still sucking occasionally on her finger. The image was so precious and melancholy at the same time. A postcard for a place she probably would never see for herself. She wished— No, it didn't matter what she wished. She had no business letting the tale unfold in her thoughts, developing it like a play with costumes, scenery and makeup. Coveting was sinful.

She slowly withdrew her finger from the baby's mouth and shuffled to the door, reluctant to hand over her little charge but resigned to doing what was right.

"Goodbye, little one." As she passed through the entry to the front porch, she placed a kiss on his fuzzy blond head. A single tear broke through her defenses and inched down her cheek.

"I don't even know your name."

"His name's Gabriel."

Detective Zach Fletcher couldn't help being curious when Pilar's head came up with a snap at his announcement. With five years under his belt as a beat cop and then another four years as a Chestnut Grove Police Department detective, Zach had developed a sixth sense about guilt, and Miss Estes had it written all over her. Only it didn't make sense because she'd been the one to report the crime. What did she have to feel guilty about?

Zach was grateful for Pilar's suspicious reaction because it distracted him from the ghosts of the past hovering in his thoughts. The whole scene felt like a cruel déjà vu, and he wasn't ready to return there. He wondered if he ever would be.

Did Pilar worry he thought the baby was hers? He almost smiled at the thought. Even if he hadn't seen Pilar at Chestnut Grove Community Church most Sundays for the last two years, he would have recognized that someone with a figure as slender as hers couldn't have been pregnant recently. And only the worst detective would have linked the fair-skinned, light-haired infant with Pilar, who had olive skin, dramatic dark eyes and long black hair, due to her Puerto Rican heritage.

"How did you beat the ambulance here?" She glanced at his car, which was parked up the street near hers. Instead of waiting for his answer, she crouched to retrieve the thick blanket from the basket and wrapped it lightly over the baby.

"I was on my way to work, caught the call on the police radio. I live close by." He chose not to mention that he couldn't have kept away if he'd been ordered to, that he had this overwhelming need to make a difference this time when he'd failed so miserably before.

"When will the ambulance arrive?"

"In a few minutes."

He checked down the street and hoped he was right. When he glanced back at Pilar, he caught her watching him with a strange expression. Was it wariness? Or curiosity?

Pilar looked away, but Zach continued to study her, for investigative purposes only. She was dressed in what he would describe as one of her trademark outfits: a ruffled, feminine blouse and a pair of tailored black slacks. Though she usually wore skirts to church, the theme was the same. It wasn't just her choice of clothes that made her look tall. She was at least five-seven in stocking feet.

Others might have been surprised that he could give such detail about a woman he didn't know well, or that he was noticing even more specifics about her now— such as her open-toe shoes and dark painted toenails— but Zach considered it his job to remember details.

What he noticed at that moment was how natural Pilar appeared, swaying with a baby she'd just discovered, literally, on the doorstep. The infant looked so comfortable sleeping there, as if this morning was like any other instead of one that would change his life.

She wrapped the blanket tightly over the baby, though she shivered herself. He was tempted to drape his herringbone sport jacket over her shoulders but worried it might offend her or make her more skittish. Her skin appeared to be the only thing keeping her from shattering into dozens of pieces.

Her uncharacteristic vulnerability surprised him. The Pilar Estes he'd observed at church had always seemed so strong, so independent. Her life and her family, all active members at their church, had appeared too perfect for the two of them to ever be friends. He'd experienced too-perfect at home and knew now what a fallacy it was.

But Zach recognized the importance of keeping a careful distance from case witnesses. He couldn't worry about Pilar right now when his focus needed to be on this new case and the abandoned infant. When he stepped closer to get a better look at the baby, he tried not to notice that Pilar took an automatic step back.

"He had a rough morning, but our little guy doesn't look too worse for the wear," he said, keeping the conversation light. "God was watching out for him."

The sides of Pilar's mouth pulled up at that. "How did you know the baby's name was Gabriel?"

"There was a note."

She seemed to accept that and didn't even ask to see it. "He probably wasn't outside too long. The mother even knew enough to swaddle him tightly so he wouldn't be able to move and maybe be smothered in the blankets."

Zach ignored the hitch in his throat and said a quick prayer of thanksgiving over the mother's insight. The situation could have been a lot uglier. "It wasn't an average person who abandoned this baby." He pointed to the blanket. "Isn't that cashmere?"

Pilar traced her finger along the stitched edge and nodded. "The basket's nice, too." She studied it for several seconds, her gaze following the intricate weaving and designs. "Maybe even an heirloom."

The wheels in Zach's brain started spinning. Clearly, the mother wasn't destitute, so what had brought her to this point? Maybe she was a wealthy, married woman who'd become pregnant from an illicit affair. He doubted that idea, as other socialites would have noticed her pregnancy during charity guild meetings and country club parties.

Maybe the mother had postpartum depression, or she was a pregnant teen with a pair of furious parents, just like Jasmine. He shook the thought away and tried to guess what the baby's mother looked like. His hands perspired with the effort. Every time he imagined a blond woman with either blue or brown eyes, the image would transform into a wavy-haired brunette with the cutest dimples and blue eyes similar to his own.

No, he couldn't think about his sister here. Not now. He didn't want to see that pair of caskets again, one white and impossibly small, and he didn't want to wonder again how he might have helped if he'd only known Jasmine's secret sooner. This time could be different. This time he could help prevent a crisis from becoming a tragedy.

"Hey, look at this." Pilar spoke just above a whisper, waving a hand for him to draw closer.

She showed him the label on Gabriel's blue sleeper. He shrugged, no fashion aficionado. He took plenty of ribbing at the station for his wardrobe choices.

Pilar pointed to the label again. "That's definitely not Ralph Lauren. The receiving blanket, too. I could buy both of those for ten dollars together at any of the local discount stores. Why would a mother who could afford cashmere choose these?"

"Maybe she couldn't." Could the blanket and basket have been products of a larceny? "I'll check back at the station to see if there were any recent B and E's—ah, breaking and entering cases—that might be related."

As if they'd called to coordinate their arrivals, the patrol car and the ambulance arrived at almost the same time from opposite directions. All the noise awakened the baby, who cried out the moment his blue eyes opened. Two emergency medical technicians emerged from the ambulance, and Pilar rushed over to them. Zach conferred for a few minutes with Officer Steve Merritt before the junior officer turned the case over to him.

After he was gone, Zach scanned the crime scene for more clues. The suspect certainly had left enough to make him wonder if she wanted to be caught. Was abandoning her child a way of crying for help? He wouldn't know until he found her, but he wanted to be that help if she needed it.

Though he tried to focus on the crime scene alone, something kept drawing his attention back to the ambulance where Pilar stood. This time she wasn't paying attention to him at all. She only had eyes for the baby who was giving the EMT hearing damage as he tried to get a heart rate.

Zach figured from the baby's healthy cry that he was going to be fine, but Pilar's expression was stark and anguished. Was that just her empathy for the baby who had lost a mother that morning?

For a few sick seconds, Zach was jealous of that baby. He wondered how it would feel to be the recipient of Pilar's empathy or her compassion. Then he grabbed hold of his wayward thoughts. He didn't need anyone to care about him. People who cared got hurt, felt losses so profoundly that their hearts seemed to have been riddled with bullets.

Though he didn't need it himself, Zach still valued the kind of compassionate care Pilar brought to her work. As a police officer, he'd seen far too few people who truly cared for their fellow human beings. The children of Tiny Blessings Adoption Agency were fortunate to have someone like Pilar on their side.

## Chapter Two

Pilar took several long, deep breaths as she waited for her world to stop spinning. The knowledge that the baby appeared healthy wasn't enough to slow this Tilt-A-Whirl she'd been riding on and couldn't get off. If she looked up the word "surreal" in the dictionary, she would find a photograph of this scene outside the Tiny Blessings building. She would see flashing lights and uniformed emergency workers and a crying baby.

And she would see the man she'd secretly mooned over for the last two years standing not ten feet away from her and still looking past her as if she was invisible. Obviously, the crisis hadn't changed anything.

She'd been overwhelmed enough just discovering the abandoned child, but that was before Zach's deep voice had rolled into her ears and jolted her pulse. He was so out of context away from the church that it had taken her a few seconds to get her bearings. Not that she wouldn't have recognized his voice anywhere, as many times as she'd overheard him talking with church friends and had wished he'd been laughing with her instead.

She glanced at him over her shoulder, careful not to get caught staring again. She'd been humiliated enough the first time. He looked so strong and proficient, taking charge of the scene and offering direction to the young uniformed police officer standing next to him. Usually the one to volunteer to head projects, Pilar felt relieved to leave the situation in Zach's capable hands.

The wind was whipping through his wavy brown hair, forcing him to shove it out of his eyes. He wore his hair a tad longer than the current extreme styles, so it fell low across his forehead and curled the tiniest bit at his nape. Zach marched to his own fashion drummer, as well, even now looking endearingly rumpled in his sport jacket matched with a pair of khaki slacks that had never known a knife crease.

When she'd already watched him longer than she should have, Zach glanced back at her. The most startling pair of cornflower-blue eyes in, well, the history of cornflower-blue eyes, trapped her in their examining stare. Her breath hitched, and goose bumps appeared on her forearms, but she couldn't look away.

At first he didn't, either—his eyes wide. What did he see when he looked at her? Just another witness to interview? A case number? A day on the job? She hoped he didn't see her yearning. She'd hidden it so well before just as all secret crushes should be carefully guarded, but her resistance was down this morning, her self-protection compromised. She exhaled when he finally looked back at his fellow police officer, but she felt oddly disappointed.

A hearty laugh pulled Pilar back to the commotion next to the ambulance.

"This one's got a pair of lungs on him," said one of the EMTs.

The other one laughed with him. "He's just offended that you're poking at him. I would be, too."

"You take him. I'll call in his vitals." Before the second guy could protest, the first was off with the radio.

Gabriel continued to wail, his face becoming reddish-purple and his feet beating against the blanket. She couldn't help smiling at him. He'd been dealt a tough blow that morning, but he was a fighter. He was going to be okay. She just knew it.

Pilar touched his head once more, her fingers tracing a path through the sweaty fuzz, and then the paramedic took him inside the ambulance. Her eyes and nose burned. She should have been praising God that little Gabriel appeared to be all right. He would be fine, and Zach would locate his mother for him. That was what she wanted, right? With surprise and a fair amount of guilt, Pilar realized she didn't want Gabriel's mother to be found.

As the ambulance pulled away from the curb, its precious cargo inside, Zach turned back to Pilar, anxiety heavy on his chest. He should have taken the easy-out clause Sergeant Roy Hollowell had offered him when he'd called in. The sergeant knew Zach's history and was trying to save him some grief by not assigning him to the case, but Zach had insisted. Now he wondered why he'd volunteered to suffer.

He scribbled again on his notepad, taking down crime scene details. Hopefully, he would find enough leads this morning to keep him busy all afternoon. He turned to Pilar, who was walking back toward him, the wind blowing dark bangs into her eyes. She shoved her hair back from her face and rubbed her hands up and down her upper arms.

This time he didn't bother worrying about offending her. Chivalry wouldn't die under his watch if he could help it.

"Here, take my jacket," he said, already descending the steps and lowering it onto her shoulders.

She started to speak, but he waved away her protests. "Don't worry about it. I need to ask you a few questions, and I don't want you to freeze while I'm doing it."

But she wasn't listening to him as her gaze was focused on his shoulder holster and the .40-caliber semiautomatic that until then had been hidden under his jacket. He asked his first question to distract her.

"Can you tell me the approximate time when you first noticed the baby?"

Pilar's head jerked until she met his gaze again. She chewed her lip for several seconds and then shook her head.

"Sorry."

"That's okay, but try to think back. Do you know how long you waited after discovering the child before you called police? Dispatch recorded your call at 0724."

Her gaze darted from the basket to the office entry and back before she turned to him, again shaking her head. Zach gripped his pen tighter but refused to become frustrated. Pilar was going to be helpful to him. He only needed to ask the right questions first.

"Let's start with something else. Did you see anyone suspicious-looking around the building just before or just after you found the victim?"

Pilar rubbed her chin and looked at the ground. For a third time, she shook her head.

Zach's jaw tightened. Was she purposely being difficult, or did she really not remember anything? From everything he'd ever sensed from or heard about the ultratogether Pilar Estes, he would have expected her to be able to relate the story in minute detail. Was she hiding something? And if so, why?

The basket drew his attention then, as full of questions as it was empty of its earlier contents.

"Can you show me exactly where you found the infant?"

This time she didn't hesitate at all. She climbed the porch steps and peered down at the open basket, the cashmere blanket folded inside it. Her posture relaxed, and she pressed her lips together as if holding back a smile. When she glanced back at him, she raised an eyebrow though she easily could have said "duh" at the lame question, worthy of a rookie cop.

*All right, Fletcher, pull it together.* Her opinion of the way he conducted the investigation shouldn't have mattered, but it did.

"Of course. The basket," he muttered. "Did you move it, or did you find it right there on the porch?"

"Right there." She studied the container for several seconds more, and then her gaze shot up. "You said there was a note. I didn't see one, but then I never thought to look for one. Where did you find it?"

Who was asking the questions now? It was his turn to raise an eyebrow. "In the basket."

She really smiled this time, an expression so warm it could have melted ice along the banks of the James River. The smile gave him the same jolt he'd experienced when he'd caught her staring earlier. She'd met his gaze squarely then and hadn't bothered to look away.

Mirth danced in her glistening black eyes now, but earlier he'd seen something else entirely in them, intense and soulful at the same time. Perhaps he'd only reacted to Pilar's need to connect with another human being on a day when she'd witnessed a tragic side of humanity, but he'd felt her reaching out to him. Stranger still, he'd been tempted to reach right back.

That fact alone should have sent him hightailing it back to the station so he could ask the sergeant to reassign the case. He didn't *do* relationships of any kind, let alone the male-female kind. He liked being alone. He was good at it. And people who were good at being alone didn't have to risk losing anyone important to them.

And yet Pilar's smile drew him in. That shouldn't have surprised him. He'd seen at church how adults and children alike gravitated toward her as she met each with her welcoming smile. This time, though, she'd directed her grin at him, and he liked that more than he cared to admit.

"Why didn't I think of looking there?" she said when the lull in the conversation stretched too long.

"You were too busy making sure the baby was okay."

"True." Her smile was gone.

Why did he suddenly want to perform clown tricks or do a stand-up routine to make her smile again? Still, he had a job to do, and he didn't have time to kid around.

"The note was buried under the blanket. We'll see if we can pull any prints from it. Want to see it?"

He slipped back on the plastic glove from his pocket and opened the brown paper sack he'd placed the letter in. He carefully unfolded the piece of thick, ecru stationery.

"It's addressed to the staff of Tiny Blessings. It says, 'Please find my baby boy Gabriel a good home full of love. And tell him I love him.'"

When Pilar didn't say anything, he decided he couldn't blame her. He was having a hard enough time scaring up sympathy for this mother who claimed to love her baby, and he didn't work in a field full of childless couples desperate to adopt. He could only imagine the mixed feelings Pilar must have felt.

"Gabriel." She nodded, her gaze distant. "It's perfect for him. He's named after an angel. You know that story, of how Gabriel appeared to Zechariah to tell him his elderly wife, Elizabeth, would have a son, right?"

Zach shot a sidelong glance at her, convinced he hadn't heard her right, but she wasn't laughing.

"The same angel who appeared to Mary later, telling her she would give birth to Jesus," he said to prove he did know what she was talking about. He wanted to ask Pilar what her point was, but he doubted she had one. Why were they reciting biblical stories when they should have been out finding Gabriel's mom and protecting her from making mistakes that couldn't be fixed?

"Yes, his name is perfect," she said, nodding her agreement with the choice.

The conversation was so strange that Zach wasn't sure how to respond. Maybe she just needed him to cut her some slack since she'd been through a harrowing morning. She wasn't herself, and probably needed a friend. Though he knew better, he was tempted to volunteer for the job.

"Pilar," he said in his gentlest voice, "you do see that Gabriel's life isn't perfect, don't you? You have to see that he needs his mother."

She stiffened and looked past him at the street, which was beginning to fill with cars as the rest of Chestnut Grove headed to work.

"She probably had very good reasons for leaving her baby," she said, but didn't sound convinced.

"We don't know what her situation is, but it's my job to find her."

"And arrest her?"

She had him there. Personally, he might want to find Gabriel's mother to make sure she was okay, but the state of Virginia wanted him to find her so it could charge her with a crime. Zach opened his mouth and closed it again. What could he say to that?

"I just wouldn't want to see her face more misery if she's located," she said. "She's done a good thing by putting her baby in place where he could be found. Now he can have that good, loving home she wrote that she wanted for him."

"But she might be in real trouble, bigger trouble than facing criminal charges. We don't know if she received proper prenatal or postnatal care or if she even delivered in a hospital."

"Zach, how do you know she even *wants* to be found?"

"She might not, you're right. But I have to find her and not just because of child welfare laws." He tried to take a breath, but his lungs only ached the same way his heart ached.

"I just don't want her to end up like—" Zach stopped himself, amazed that he'd been about to say "Jasmine." He'd told no one about his past, except his superiors at work, and he'd only informed them out of necessity. It was too painful, too private. Yet he'd nearly bared his scars to someone he hardly knew. What was wrong with him?

"Like what?" Pilar asked.

Zach shook his head. It was so clear that he shouldn't have taken the assignment. If he had any sense at all, he would go back to the station and ask for it to be reassigned. But he wouldn't, because to him this was more than an assignment. He felt a calling here to help, no matter how much it hurt. He might be the only chance that Gabriel's mother had.

*Lord, please give me the strength to do the right thing. Please be with the baby's mother. Show her that You care and that others care, too.* Zach would have said "Amen," but he got the feeling this situation was going to require a lot more prayers.

"Like what?" Pilar asked a second time, apparently guessing he hadn't heard her.

"Like other women who've made mistakes."

He would have explained that he, like her, wanted the situation to be okay for the baby and for his mother, if Kelly Young hadn't rushed up the sidewalk then, her long dress coat fluttering behind her like a superhero's cape.

"Why was the ambulance here? Is there anything wrong? Are you all right?" Her multitoned blond hair fluttered in the wind as she peppered Pilar with questions.

Zach stepped forward to take charge as he was accustomed to doing, but Pilar, her posture straight, moved past him to the agency's director. The jacket he'd placed around Pilar's shoulders was now draped over her arm.

"Everything's fine, Kelly. I just found an abandoned baby on the steps this morning."

"Just?" Kelly's eyes were wide as she repeated Pilar's word. "You *just* found an abandoned baby? This is all we need."

Pilar looked back and forth between them. "Uh, Kelly Young, this is Zach Fletcher, a detective from the Chestnut Grove Police Department."

Zach nodded at the always-professional director. "Miss Young."

"Detective Fletcher," Kelly responded before turning to Pilar. "We've met."

Pilar breathed in suddenly as she realized how the two had met—first during the investigation concerning the falsified birth records discovered at the agency, and again following the recent arson and vandalism investigation. As much of a revolving door as Tiny Blessings had been for police personnel the last two months, it surprised Zach that he and Pilar hadn't crossed paths there before.

Distress still lined Pilar's face, but Kelly showed no outward sign of it. Just as she had during the earlier investigations, Kelly Young appeared professionally concerned but personally untouched by the surrounding chaos. Figuring the director was probably like him, adept at detaching herself from things that might clutter up her emotions, he filled her in on the details.

"We're not sure how long the infant was on the step before Miss Estes arrived."

How strange that he was back in his distant professional mode, when earlier he'd called Pilar by her first name. He offered the excuse that all members of their church were on a first-name basis, but even he didn't buy it.

"The infant is being taken to Children's Hospital in Richmond," he explained.

Kelly didn't say anything, seeming to quietly absorb the information.

Pilar rested a hand on her boss's shoulder. "Don't worry. I think everything's going to be fine. The baby—his name is Gabriel—seems healthy. The Department of Children and Families will find him a good home."

Zach figured that if the director was worried about anything under all that composure, it would have involved damage control, rather than the foundling's health and prospects. Pilar, on the other hand, seemed too intent on adopting out the baby before he even had a chance to locate the mother.

"We're still a long way from that happening," he reminded her, but wasn't sure she was listening.

He let Pilar fill Kelly in on the rest of the story, listening in case she revealed more details she'd neglected to tell him. Still, the director remained calm, though even he recognized that the last thing the agency needed was to end up in the news again.

"I thought I might visit the hospital later today, just to make sure the baby is okay," Pilar was saying as Zach tuned back into the conversation.

"Sounds like a good idea," Kelly said before turning to Zach. "Is there anything else you'll need from us?"

"Not at the moment. But I'll probably want to talk to Miss Estes again after I've followed up on a few leads."

With a quick glance toward her boss, Pilar handed his jacket back to him. "Thanks for that."

Kelly looked back and forth between them but didn't say anything.

"Sure thing." After slipping his jacket back on and adjusting his shoulder holster, Zach pulled a business card from his pocket and handed it to Pilar. "You'll call me if you think of anything else, won't you?"

He offered a hand, and she took it. Her hands were small and soft, but her grip was sure and firm, like the woman he'd imagined her to be. He couldn't imagine, however, why he was reluctant to let her go.

Because thoughts like that were unacceptable in the safe world he'd created for himself, Zach did release her hand and moved on to shake hands with Kelly. He needed to put some distance between himself and these people as soon as possible. Bending, he retrieved the basket and headed down the walk.

Like the unwanted publicity for Tiny Blessings, there were plenty of things in this world over which none of them had control. Illegal activities that occurred at an agency before most of the current staff were born. A sister whose loss was neither explainable nor forgivable. Even mothers whose lives reached some desperation point where abandoning their children seemed like the only alternative.

Zach could do nothing about any of these things, but there was one thing he could do, and he refused to stop until he'd finished the job. He was going to find little Gabriel's mother.

## Chapter Three

Kelly closed the door to her office and slumped behind the desk, able to breathe for the first time since she'd driven up the street toward work. Nothing like seeing an ambulance in front of her office, its lights flashing and siren blaring, to get the old blood pumping. What now? she'd wondered then. Now she just wondered why so many.rotten things had to happen at one place.

Her biggest mistake wasn't in assuming that the situation at work couldn't get any worse. It was getting out of bed today at all.

"Why here?"

But even as she spoke the question aloud to her office's four walls, she knew the answer. She worked at an adoption agency after all. Many people probably assumed that a private adoption agency could take in a foundling and find him a good home. Few knew that the duty fell to the Department of Children and Families.

Kelly cringed over the publicity that was sure to come. Local reporter Jared Kierney probably would jump on this in a minute. Even if he took the human-interest angle, the agency couldn't bear more attention, especially anything associated with a crime.

Tiny Blessings had seen enough print the last several weeks to last a lifetime. First, there was the story Jared had broken about the falsified birth records she, Pilar and Anne Smith had found behind that false wall in the office.

Kelly gritted her teeth and wished again that she had fired the office cleaning lady, Florence Villi, months before she'd had the chance to leak that information to the press. But the front-page article about the arson fire that destroyed most of those records topped even that.

She could just imagine this newest headline: Baby Found. Discovery Adds to Agency's Woes. She might as well kiss new donations goodbye after all this, and as a nonprofit organization, Tiny Blessings couldn't afford to lose a single gift. Who could blame the *Richmond Gazette* for publishing the articles, though? Scandal made for good copy, and it sold newspapers.

Still, it broke her heart to think of the huge black mark Barnaby Harcourt had painted on the agency's reputation. For the right price, he'd helped wealthy families make their daughters' problems *go away* through illegal adoptions. She still couldn't understand how the money was worth violating the public trust. Tiny Blessings had done so much good over the years, placing children in wonderful, loving families. She ought to know—she was one of the first children placed by the agency.

Someone knocked on the door just as a shaky feeling settled inside her and goose bumps appeared on her arms. She needed to get control of her emotions. Allowing this situation to become personal would be a mistake, and she couldn't let that happen. She had a job to do, and she would do it, no questions asked.

"Yes?" She pulled the sweater off the back of her office chair and draped it across her shoulders.

Pilar entered the office. "Hey." She stepped inside and closed the door behind her.

Neither needed to point out the subtle workplace difference that morning. On ordinary days, Kelly's office door was open unless she was meeting with adoptive parents or a mother considering adoption as an alternative. This would be no ordinary day for anyone at the office.

"Sorry, I didn't get the coffee made," Pilar said as she slipped into the chair opposite her boss's desk.

Kelly laughed, appreciating Pilar, who was always trying to make those around her feel better. "Well, could you get on it?"

"Right away, boss." But Pilar stayed seated.

Neither of them needed caffeine to wake up this morning, anyway. With her rolling stomach, Kelly doubted she would be able to choke down even half a cup.

"Some morning, huh?" Pilar said finally.

"That's the understatement of the year." Kelly took in the way Pilar was wringing her hands. "You okay?"

"Yeah, I'm fine. A little shaken is all."

Shell-shocked was more like it, but Kelly didn't call her on it. "I'll write up a press release this morning. I'm also going to have to give Jared that interview he's been begging for." She shook her head. "And to think that last year we were dying for publicity."

Again, the room grew silent as each curled into her own thoughts. But Pilar leaned forward and rested her forearms on Kelly's desk.

"What about you? Are you okay?"

"Why wouldn't I be? I wasn't the one who just found a baby—"

"You know what I mean. Did it make you wonder about your birth mother?"

Kelly shook her head, but straightened in her chair. "Of course not."

For the umpteenth time, she wished she'd been alone when she'd come across her own altered birth records, and her friend Ben Cavanaugh's, among the dozens in the hidden box. It was information she'd never needed nor wanted to know, and she wished her employees didn't know it, either.

Marcus and Carol Young were her parents, and that was that. She'd had the most perfect childhood a person could ever ask for, and she never would have betrayed their memory by digging up the past. Unfortunately, that past had resurfaced without any help from her.

"I just hope baby Gabriel's okay."

Pilar might as well have slugged Kelly, as effectively as her words knocked the wind out of her. How could she have only been thinking about their agency and her personal mess when that baby had lost his mother that morning?

She concentrated on Pilar, who was staring out the office window toward Main Street, though from that seated position she couldn't have seen anything outside. For someone with olive skin, she appeared pale. She gripped and ungripped her hands.

"You're more than a little shaken, aren't you?"

At least Pilar didn't bother to deny it this time. The corners of her mouth turned up in what could barely be called a smile.

Kelly reached across the desk and squeezed both of her hands. "He'll be fine. How can he not be? He was already fortunate enough to have been left on the steps for an early riser like you."

Pulling her hands away, Pilar rubbed her upper arms as if she'd become chilled. "I just can't stop imagining what might have happened to him if I hadn't gotten there. If he'd been out there, exposed to the elements, where just anyone could have taken him."

"But it didn't happen that way. He's safe now and in capable hands. Detective Fletcher will have the case under control in no time."

Pilar stiffened, her hands becoming still on her arms. After several seconds, she glanced across the desk, her expression too casual. "You think so?"

Kelly thought something, all right. She'd had a fleeting suspicion earlier, but now she was convinced. Why had Pilar been wearing Zach's jacket in the first place? And why had she been uncomfortable returning it with Kelly there?

"He's a great detective." Still, she couldn't resist adding, "He'll probably need to ask you more questions about the case, though."

"Oh."

*Oh* was right. Biting her lip, Kelly managed not to laugh. In the whole time Pilar had worked at Tiny Blessings, she'd gone on maybe a handful of dates, and it was a pretty empty hand at that. She was pleased to realize her friend wasn't immune to the handsome Detective Fletcher.

As immediately after work as she could without leaving before five or speeding, Pilar arrived at the door of the downtown tri-level that felt as comfortable to her as her parents' home.

The warmth that poured out of the place the moment Naomi Fraser opened the glass storm door made Pilar smile. Naomi's vivid blue eyes glistened in the late-afternoon sun as she nabbed Pilar for a not-so-quick hug against her pillow-soft body.

"You sure made it here fast."

"Traffic was good," Pilar managed to get out, still enclosed in that warm embrace. If there had been traffic tie-ups she might have been tempted to drive on the sidewalk, but Pilar didn't tell the minister's wife that.

Naomi let go in her own sweet time and took a step back as if to appraise her guest. She shook her head, her no-nonsense short haircut fluttering and falling back into place, and gave Pilar one more squeeze for good measure.

That Naomi always hugged like she meant it was one of the things Pilar adored about the woman she'd known since her days on the church's infant cradle roll. There were plenty of other reasons to like someone who wore pearls with blue jeans and never sugarcoated the truth, but Pilar liked the hugs best. And it was a well-known fact that one of the best advertisements Reverend John Fraser had for his church was his redheaded darling of a wife.

"Good traffic is a blessing, and so are babies." Naomi's eyes danced with excitement as she led Pilar to the dark-paneled family room and gestured toward the portable crib in the corner. "You were right—he's a baby doll."

Her pulse racing, Pilar could barely restrain herself from sprinting over to the crib, grabbing Gabriel and holding him against her heart. She forced herself to slow down by studying the Frasers' clean but lived-in house. The stacks of books, Bibles and crossword puzzle magazines, so different from her mother's immaculate home, made the room seem as relaxed as the family itself.

, Proud of herself for her control, Pilar finally was close enough to peek over the edge of the crib's mesh side. Gabriel lay there on his back, with one arm he'd freed from his swaddling blanket pressed against his jaw. Until her lungs started aching, Pilar didn't even realize she'd been holding her breath. She exhaled it slowly.

"He's beautiful, isn't he?" Naomi asked.

*And alone,* she wanted to add, but she only nodded. When she couldn't resist any longer, she reached over the side of the crib to brush his damp hair. He slept so soundly that he didn't move, except for the even rise and fall of his chest.

Naomi stepped close and whispered, "He's been sleeping like that almost since he got here. Those doctors probably wore him out."

"They said he was all right, didn't they?" Her question sounded too sharp in her ears.

"Of course," Naomi said, though she studied her for a few seconds. "He's a perfectly healthy baby boy. And really new, too—no more than a few days."

"I still can't believe Gabriel ended up here. I was so surprised when you mentioned it on the phone earlier."

"It shouldn't surprise you too much," Reverend Fraser said as he crossed from the kitchen back to his study, a handful of chocolate chip cookies in his grip. His wire-rim glasses were perched on his nose like always, but he wasn't wearing his clerical collar.

"We've been licensed foster parents almost ten years now. Somebody's always coming or going through that door."

He pointed to the mantel and to the wall collages where photographs of John and Naomi's two adult children, Jonah and Dinah, and teenage daughter, Ruth, shared space with pictures of at least thirty other children.

"But not—" Pilar stopped herself before saying "my baby," but just barely. "Not the baby I found."

The minister's dark brown eyes peered at her over the tops of his glasses before he smiled.

"You're right. He is a rare one."

Patting Pilar's shoulder as he passed, he stopped at the side of the crib. "Now that's a fine-looking fellow if I ever saw one." With a wave he slipped into his study, leaving the door open a crack.

"Mom, do I get to hold the new baby before practice?" Sixteen-year-old Ruth Fraser chased her question into the room in a blur of bright copper hair and red-and-black pom-poms. When she noticed Pilar there, she gave the same electric smile she must have offered the judges for her competitive cheerleading competitions.

"Hey, Pilar. Did I hear you found Gabriel in a cabbage patch?"

Pilar grinned at the brown-eyed, freckled teen who shared her mother's exuberance. "No, on a doorstep. He stayed a lot cleaner that way."

As if he recognized he was center of discussion, Gabriel started grunting and wiggling in his blanket. His eyes popped open. Naomi bent to lift him from the crib and rested him against her shoulder. Ruth held out her arms, pom-poms dangling from her hands, but Naomi waved her off.

"You've got about ten minutes to pick up your room before practice. You'll have plenty of time to hold him later, after prayer meeting." Naomi winked at her daughter. "Since Gabriel's going to be up all night, you can have the three o'clock shift."

"Gee, thanks, Mom." She frowned and then grinned. "Didn't Dinah volunteer for the night shift?"

"Eeeee. Wrong answer. Your sister won't even get off work at the grocery store until eleven, and she might get called to substitute teach in the morning."

"She gets all the breaks."

"I'll be sure to tell her that," Naomi said brightly. "Now, are you going? Your room isn't getting any cleaner while we're chatting."

Ruth tilted her head to the side. "Can I take the minivan?"

"If you remember to put gas in it this time," Reverend Fraser called from the other room.

"I'll try, Dad."

"Don't try. Succeed." He closed the door, probably to finish his Sunday sermon.

"See you at church," Ruth called as she jogged to the kitchen for the car keys. "Don't forget to pick up Tori from play practice."

"I won't forget." At Pilar's questioning look, Naomi explained. "Victoria St. Claire. You've probably seen her one of these past few Sundays. She's been here about a month. She's fourteen and about as boy-crazy as Ruth."

"Is that possible?" Pilar chuckled, having heard stories about Ruth's antics before.

The laughter died in her throat the moment that Naomi lowered Gabriel into Pilar's arms. Emotion lodged in her throat instead, heavy and full.

"Hey, little one, you remember Pilar, don't you?" Naomi spoke in a singsongy voice as she brushed a finger down the baby's forehead. "You two are old friends."

Pilar's heart squeezed as she cradled the sleep-warmed body. All day at work her thoughts had been like a game of keep-away, jumping from Gabriel to Zach to her upcoming surgery and back to Zach, but she couldn't catch them and subdue them so she could get some work done.

The unsettled feeling she'd been battling, though, evaporated as soon as she inhaled Gabriel's fresh baby scent. Holding him felt so natural, as if he belonged there, close enough to her heart to hear its calming rhythm. For several seconds, the baby simply stared up at her.

"He likes you," Naomi observed. "We'll probably have him here for a while, so feel free to visit him whenever you like. I'm sure he would enjoy some spoiling."

Whenever she liked? "I'll do that."

The baby started wiggling and smacking his lips, so Pilar propped him against her shoulder and walked around the room. "Do you want me to give him a bottle?"

"Sure, just a minute. I'll warm one up."

As soon as Naomi disappeared into the kitchen, the doorbell rang. Naomi's voice could be heard from the other room. "Ruth, could you—"

"I'll get it," Ruth called as she tromped down the stairs. Muffled voices filtered from the entry and then stopped.

"Bye, Mom and Dad." The door closed again.

In the silence that filled the family room, Pilar focused on little Gabriel alone. "You're going to be just fine, sweetheart," she said softly. "Dinner's on the way. You don't have to be cold here, or hungry or lonely. You'll be happy here until we find you a new home."

She stopped crooning to him just as Naomi came down the hall.

The veteran mom tested the formula's temperature on the inside of her forearm as she approached. "Who was at the door?"

"Ruth never said. Must have been a salesman or something." She reached for the bottle Naomi had been extending, but Naomi suddenly pulled back.

"Hi." She spoke to someone over Pilar's shoulder. "If I'd known there was going to be a party, I would have put on a pot of chili and some hot dogs."

Pilar expected to hear laughter from the reverend or one of their children, since Naomi was a notoriously bad cook whose chili had a reputation all its own. But the sound that skittered up Pilar's back and rolled over her shoulder in baritone richness hadn't come from anyone living in the Fraser household.

"Don't go to any trouble cooking on my account."

Pilar whirled to find Zach leaning against the doorway, his arms folded and his ankles crossed as if he'd been there for a while. Her mouth went dry, and her cheeks burned. Just how long had he been watching? What had he overheard? And why had he been listening anyway?

"Just thought I'd drop by for a few minutes," Zach said to Naomi, never taking his eyes off Pilar. His smile was slow and deliberate. He'd caught her, and they both knew it. So often Pilar had dreamed of having Zach stare at her, and now she only felt trapped by his study.

Handing the bottle to Pilar, Naomi marched over to Zach and gave him the hug treatment. Apparently, she'd missed whatever had passed between the other two adults.

"What were you doing sneaking in on us like that?" Naomi asked as she released him.

"I didn't sneak. Ruth let me in," he said, still looking at Naomi's other guests.

Pilar popped the bottle between the baby's lips, and he went to work on it, a good portion of the formula dripping down his chin. She didn't want Zach to witness her inexperience in caring for a child, yet she sensed his gaze on her.

"We'll have to work on our daughter's manners," Naomi was saying. "I'm surprised she didn't stay to visit."

Zach grinned. Ruth's crush on him had hardly been

a secret, and though he'd done nothing to encourage it, he'd always been kind to the teen.

"You didn't say you'd be coming by." Naomi had a strange expression on her face when Zach finally turned to face her.

"Oh, I was talking to the reverend earlier, and he told me the infant Doe has come to stay. I wanted to drop by to see how he's getting along."

"He's doing great," Pilar answered, finding her voice for the first time since seeing Zach.

"That's good. I've got some solid leads. I've got a good feeling about this investigation. I'm going to find his mother."

Zach glanced down at the baby for a few seconds before meeting Pilar's gaze again. "It's good to see you here, too. I wanted to ask you a few more questions."

Naomi stepped forward then, reaching for the baby. Already he'd drunk down most of the four-ounce bottle.

"Here, let me take Gabriel up for a burp and a change. You two sit on the couch so Zach can ask his questions. When I get back down, I'll let Zach hold Gabriel." Wearing a Cheshire-cat smile, she didn't wait for an answer before moving toward the stairs.

Pilar sat opposite Zach, pushing her back against the sofa arm. If only the piece of furniture could grow longer so she could move farther away from his intense stare. She could remember final exams in college where she'd been far less nervous than at this moment. Why did he keep staring at her as if she was a criminal?

She cleared her throat. "You said you want to ask me some questions."

"I do."

But he didn't. He just continued to watch her until she couldn't take it anymore.

"Did you come to use strange interrogation tactics on me? Because I've already told you everything I know."

He raised an eyebrow. "Everything?"

Annoyance filled her chest. And to think she'd once been very interested in this man! She'd liked him a lot better when he was a stranger. "Yes, everything."

When he still didn't say anything, Pilar had had enough. "If you're not going to ask a question, then I am. What are you doing here, Zach?"

"I was wondering the same thing about you."

"Well, I'm here to check on Gabriel. You heard me say earlier that I was going to visit the hospital. Well, the doctors discharged him. He was placed with the Frasers, and I just wanted to make sure he's all right."

Zach tucked his chin between his index finger and thumb, contemplating her answer. "Sounds reasonable. I already told you I was here to check on the baby, too."

"Then are we done? Have you asked all your questions?"

He shook his head. "Just one more."

She waited, bearing his scrutiny for a few seconds

longer. Why did it feel as if all the walls she'd built to mask her heart's secret longings were only transparent screens to him? That though they were nearly strangers, he knew her better than almost anyone.

"Tell me this. What's the connection between you and that baby?"

# *Chapter Four*

"What do you mean, what's my connection?" Pilar asked, her eyes wide.

She was pressed so hard against the sofa arm that Zach wondered if she planned to escape over the top. He trapped her with his gaze in the way he'd learned to make lesser suspects squirm.

"That's what I'm asking. You probably place babies all the time. Do you get this attached to all of them? Or is there something different about this baby?"

When she didn't answer immediately, he continued to stare. Strange, but he hoped for Pilar's sake that she didn't have that same intense connection with each child she placed, because he didn't like the idea of her heart breaking all the time. But then he hadn't done a good job of keeping his professional distance in this case, either.

He couldn't say he'd been soft on questioning Pilar. In fact, he was grateful Naomi hadn't held him under the same level of scrutiny when she'd asked why he'd visited that day. Sure he'd come to see Gabriel, but he was beginning to wonder if the possibility of seeing Pilar again had also played into his decision.

It had certainly been for her benefit that he'd talked up the investigation when he still didn't know if any of his "solid leads" would pan out. He didn't know why it mattered so much to him that she thought he was a good detective. He'd never worried before what anyone thought as long as he was doing his best to help people. It was a good policy, and he would do well to stick to it instead of trying to impress anyone.

But this was about more than impressing. It was about curiosity, and everyone knew what that did to the cat. Pilar had become such a puzzle to him, full of challenging, interlocking pieces, when before he'd barely noticed her. Or at least when he had noticed, he'd taken in her flawless beauty and too-perfect background and had kept his distance.

"Gabriel's different," she answered finally.

"How is he different?"

Pilar blew out an exasperated breath. "I found him. He's—"

She cut herself off then, but that only made Zach want to know more. Had she nearly said "mine"? That didn't make any sense, though it did take finders-keepers to a whole new level. "He's what?"

"He's just a sweet little baby who could use all the friends he could get."

He nodded. That was true enough, but if it was what she'd intended to say, then why hadn't she looked at him when she'd said it? Her posture was stiff, and her closed body language signaled she wasn't telling the truth, the whole truth and nothing but the truth, so help her God. She was still hiding something.

Twice now he'd witnessed private moments between Pilar and the infant she should have met only that morning—first on the agency steps and now in the Frasers' family room. There was a connection, all right, but what?

Could Pilar have been a friend of Gabriel's biological mother and was covering for her? Zach pondered the premise that would have explained why she was reluctant to help with the investigation, but he couldn't buy it. As a Tiny Blessings employee, she would have encouraged the mother to give the child up for adoption, or at the very least would have *discouraged* her from breaking the law.

His gut told him Pilar's reasons were much more personal. That he could relate to. Everyone had a right to a few secrets—those personal parts that no one needed to know and that only reopened old wounds in the retelling. Did Pilar have wounds she needed to protect?

Immediately, he was contrite for the high-pressure interview tactic. Though Gabriel had more to complain about, Pilar had been through a rough day. He'd seen her that morning, had witnessed her shock and even had wrapped his jacket around her. The last thing she needed was some overzealous detective shoving her around for new leads.

"Is this the first time you've dealt with a child-abandonment case?" he asked, though he'd already guessed that it was.

She nodded. "I work with people who would give everything they have to have a child of their own. None of them would ever dump a baby, in a fancy basket or not."

He'd been right: It was personal. How could he, of anyone, criticize someone who took her job and the people it affected personally? That would be like smashing the image of the person he saw in the mirror every morning.

"Do you have a long waiting list of people hoping to adopt?"

Pilar tilted her head to study him, appearing to recognize that his question had no bearing on the case.

"We have more homes than we have children to fill them. Especially for clients who want babies. The waiting list for a newborn is often three years deep."

Zach couldn't imagine what that was like, the bureaucracy and the waiting and hoping for a child that most couples assumed would be the natural next step in their relationships. Life had no guarantees; he'd learned that the hard way. Apparently, Pilar's clients had swallowed their own bitter pills.

When he looked up again, Pilar was studying him.

"Are you finished asking questions?"

"Sure. For now."

As finished as he could be given that she hadn't really answered the important one. She'd never explained her connection to the foundling.

She nodded but didn't look him in the eye. "Well, if there's nothing else, I need to get going."

Pushing herself over the arm of the sofa, she stood as if she couldn't get away from him fast enough. He was used to women's attention, had even learned to ignore it most of the time, so he wondered why her pariah treatment bothered him so much.

Zach hesitated, which was about as unlike him as letting himself be distracted when he was on a case. He should have been telling her not to let the door slam when she left, but here he was hoping to keep her around a few minutes longer so he could prove he wasn't a bad guy. How pitiful was that?

Naomi's louder-than-necessary footsteps on the stairs saved him from a thorough self-lecture. He stood in time to see her reentering the room, carrying a clean and content baby.

"Pilar, you're not leaving, are you? I thought you were staying so we could go to prayer meeting together."

"I was, but…" Pilar paused and cleared her throat "…I've decided to meet you there."

Naomi turned to Zach. "You'll be there, won't you?"

"Not this time, sweetheart."

Naomi stuck out her lip. "But even police detectives get time off for Wednesday night prayer meeting."

"I'll have plenty of time off when Gabriel's mother has been located." He looked at Pilar to let her know that the message was for her. No matter what she was hiding or how badly he felt for her for having made this difficult discovery, he still had a job to do. With or without her help, he was going to solve this case.

Pilar made a show of studying her watch, but he was pretty sure she'd received the message.

Naomi cleared her throat. "At least let me get you some dinner." She turned back to Pilar. "You, too. It won't take me a minute to whip up a big pot of chili."

"That's okay," Zach and Pilar chorused and then shot glances at each other.

She was chewing her lower lip to keep from laughing, so he spoke for the both of them. "Thank you for the offer, but can we take a rain check?"

Naomi's sly grin suggested she was as aware as anyone of her cooking weakness. "Okay, it's a date. The kids will love having the both of you to dinner."

Date? He started. Why did he feel as if he'd just been swindled? He opened his mouth to object and caught Pilar's profile in his peripheral vision. Her mouth was open to say something, too.

Their minister's wife stopped the both of them with a wave of her hand. "I'll let you know when. I'll see you out now."

Only a few minutes later, he was buckling the seat belt of his sedan and wondering at how easily Naomi had dismissed them. It was probably for the best, he thought, as he watched Pilar climb into her red coupe.

He needed to avoid distractions if he was going to solve this case, and Pilar had become one.

Even now his thoughts flicked to the scene between Pilar and Gabriel when she'd whispered promises that she would keep him safe. Strange how he could almost see a better world when looking at it through Pilar's eyes. He saw hope, even though life had given him every reason to doubt.

He shook his head to dismiss the image now, as he had when he'd witnessed it. Some police detective he'd turned out to be. He'd been so entranced watching Pilar and her tiny charge that if Naomi hadn't announced his presence, he might have gone right on watching without thinking once about the case.

Pilar was a distraction, all right, one that neither he nor the case could afford. He wished she would just tell him what she knew so he could steer clear of her until the investigation was complete. Even after that, if he had any sense.

No one who brought out such conflicting feelings in him could be good for his life—work or otherwise. Part of him wanted to lock her in a holding cell until she told him what he wanted to know. The other, more dangerous part of him wanted to take her in his arms and tell her everything would be all right.

Pilar peered into the oval window in the Starlight Diner's front door before she pulled it open. Sure enough, Anne had already commandeered their usual booth and was sitting on one of its bright blue vinyl seats studying a menu she should have known by heart. In fact, the names Pilar Estes, Anne Smith, Meg Talbot Kierney and Rachel Noble all should have been engraved on the table's Formica top as many years as they'd been coming to the Starlight for Sunday brunch.

"Hey, Pilar," Anne called as her golden blond head came up and she set aside the menu. She would order her usual double bacon cheeseburger and fries when the waitress came anyway, and, as usual, she wouldn't pack an ounce on her slender frame.

"Hi." Pilar slid past the chrome counter, the upholstered bar stools and the black-and-white stills of Elvis Presley and Marilyn Monroe, pausing only to salute a picture of James Dean from *Giant* before she reached the booth.

"Glad to see you didn't forget to say hello to our Jimmy Dean," Anne said, glancing past her friend to the glass front door. "You're the first one here from the church crowd." She said it with laughter in her voice that almost masked the hurt.

As she slid across the smooth vinyl that caught her skirt and twisted it, Pilar studied her friend. Sunday brunches had probably become strange for Anne these last few months. Before, she'd had Meg and Rachel to help her stake a claim on their regular table, with only Pilar arriving after church. Now Meg and her new husband, Jared, were members of Chestnut Grove, and Rachel had been attending services with her fiancé, Eli

Cavanaugh, most often snuggling Rachel's adopted baby sister, Gracie, between them.

Anne probably felt a little jealous over Meg and Rachel finding love. Thoughts like that even had crossed Pilar's mind a time or two. But did Anne also feel resentful over their new church involvement? Did she wonder if she was missing something the rest of them had found?

"Good afternoon, ladies," waitress Miranda Jones said as she carried a heavy food tray to a table at the opposite end of the diner. "Be right with you."

"No rush. We're still waiting."

"I know," Miranda said over her shoulder, the tight twist that held her dark brown hair bobbing with her nod. "Two more friends."

Anne returned Pilar's sad look when their gazes caught. They were still getting used to Miranda waiting on them, wearing a pink apron that matched Sandra Lange's except for the missing script *S* at the shoulder.

Usually the diner owner made a point of waiting on "the Sunday four," as she called them herself. Now their friend was battling breast cancer and had taken several weeks off while she underwent chemotherapy. Without closing her eyes, Pilar said another quick prayer for Sandra's recovery.

"How'd you get here so fast, Miss Pilar?" Meg called as she pushed through the door, shoving her sunglasses into her curly red hair. "Did you sneak out before the youth minister's benediction?"

"I heard every last word of Caleb Williams's none-too-brief prayer, but then I didn't have to stay to greet everyone with my handsome new husband, either."

Meg chuckled at that, her pale blue eyes dancing with mirth. "Hey, you have to show off a good thing."

Anne shook her head but smiled. "What's Jared doing with the twins this afternoon?"

"Same thing he always does. He and Chance and Luke always share a 'man' lunch with peanut-butter-and-banana sandwiches and cheese curls. But they always save room for ice cream."

"As it should be," Pilar said with a nod. "Jared is such a great guy, Meg."

"If we're listing the good ones, don't forget Eli," said Rachel as she entered the restaurant and the conversation at the same time. "Can you believe we're getting married in less than three weeks? I keep thinking I'm forgetting some of the wedding details, but then I remember that God's in control and everything will be all right."

Pilar looked over her shoulder to confirm Rachel was still wearing her chestnut hair in a tight bun. Otherwise she would have been worried that someone was impersonating one of her best friends.

Snickers from the women sitting across from her suggested they'd noticed a change in their analytical friend, too. Love clearly agreed with her.

"What are you guys laughing at?" Rachel asked,

though the smile never left her lips. She slipped into the remaining space in the booth.

"Not *at,* sweetie. *With.* We're laughing *with* you," Anne said as she continued to demonstrate.

Meg cleared her throat. "Speaking of great guys, isn't Zach Fletcher investigating the abandoned-baby case?"

Pilar sucked in a breath and crossed her arms over her abdomen that had suddenly cramped. How had she forgotten, even for a short while—Gabriel's mother, the ultrasound, the whole mess? It had just been so easy to get caught up in her friends' happiness, even in Anne's loneliness, when it allowed her to forget her own problems for a few minutes.

She had taken the time as a welcome reprieve after having tried to keep thoughts of the whole mess at bay during Reverend Fraser's sermon on spiritual gifts. Church should have comforted her, but all the sights and sounds had only upset her more.

Families with small children had crowded the church's pews, so sweet in their collective worship and so clear a reminder of what she might never have. Even Gabriel was there, sleeping in Naomi's arms until he'd awakened with the realization that he hadn't had a proper meal in a few hours. Pilar had wished she could have been the one attending to his needs then, but was comforted knowing she'd get the chance to see him later that afternoon.

By themselves, those distractions would have been enough to keep her from concentrating on the sermon, but Zach's attention had pushed her right over the edge. Every time she'd glanced at him, he'd been watching, scrutinizing.

Not so long ago she would have given anything for Zach to see her, really see her, instead of just looking past, but today she'd wanted to escape his careful study. She didn't like the way she felt as if he could see right through her, could see just how empty she was inside.

"May I take your order, please?" Miranda's familiar voice filtered into Pilar's consciousness.

Already four sweating glasses of ice water rested on the table on top of their paper place mats. When no one ordered, Pilar glanced at the women seated around her. Their questioning gazes were nearly as intense as Zach's. Close, but nothing could match his.

Anne cleared her throat and turned to the waitress. "I'll have a double bacon cheeseburger and fries."

"Glad to see something around here hasn't changed. That and Isaac in the kitchen," Meg said. She waved at Isaac Tubman, the gruff but lovable cook behind the counter, before turning back to the waitress. "Hi, Miranda. How's Daniel doing?"

"He keeps me in my running shoes." The single mom grinned, her busy kindergartner clearly on her mind.

After everyone had ordered and Miranda had walked away, three pairs of eyes returned their attention to Pilar.

Rachel lifted a carefully shaped brow. "Spill, girl-friend."

Spill. Did her friends have any idea how much she wanted to do just that? To unload and fall on the support of three people she could always count on to catch her? But she just couldn't. She couldn't speak aloud the possibilities for Tuesday's appointment. That would make them real.

"Give her a break, guys. She had enough interviews this week from Detective Fletcher," Anne said, coming to her rescue. "Remember, it's not every day when you discover a foundling on your way to work. If it were that easy to find babies, everyone would be doing it."

Anne paused and smiled at Pilar. "Seriously, though, this was an awful shock for her."

Pilar stalled by taking a sip of her ice water, waiting until she could find her voice. "It was a rough week." This new week would be rougher, but she couldn't make those words come.

Anne blew out a breath. "You can say that again, sister. It's been hard for all of us at Tiny Blessings. The only one who isn't showing strain is Kelly. She seems so unshakable."

Meg rubbed her finger down the condensation on the water glass and then set it aside. "She would have to be as director of that agency. Can anything else bad happen there?"

"Can and probably will," Rachel quipped.

Anne shook her head. "Thank you for your input, Miss Sunshine."

Meg frowned. "It sure does seem as if Tiny Blessings is having more than its share of misfortune lately."

"And bad publicity," Anne added. "I had always heard there wasn't such a thing, but believe me, there is."

"I'm so sorry," Meg said, lowering her head. "You know Jared is only doing his job."

Pilar reached over and touched her hand. "Of course he is. He's only reporting the news. You'll want to tell him, though, that Kelly's ready to give him that interview he's been asking for."

"Good. It might help relieve people's minds. I feel bad about it, but as much as we love the twins, Jared and I would worry right now about recommending Tiny Blessings to other adoptive parents."

It hurt her to hear her friend say that, but she still wanted to assuage Meg's guilt. "Don't worry. You'll feel comfortable recommending it again soon. God has a plan here."

Strange, though Pilar had believed her words as she'd spoken them, she suddenly felt no more certain of their truth than she was of a positive outcome for her ultrasound. What was wrong with her? When had the faith she'd always envisioned as a cement wall around her cracked at its foundation?

"Now that sounds like our Pilar," Rachel said with a smile. "At first, I thought there might be something else wrong beyond that whole business about finding the baby."

"Or it could have been about that cute detective," Meg added. "You've always had a thing for Zach Fletcher."

Pilar grinned. "Remind me why I ever told you that."

"Because you tell us everything, and you know it," Rachel chimed in.

She did know it. That's why it was so hard to explain her hesitation in telling them about the sad possibilities weighing on her mind. She wanted to tell, needed it as much as she needed relief from this swirl of confusion.

Again she hesitated, this time long enough for the food to come and for the moment to pass. So she kept her problem bottled up inside where it could only fester until she was sure she would explode.

Before she knew it, they were sharing hugs all around and planning where to meet at the Labor Day barbecue. If only Monday didn't have to be a holiday. If only she didn't have to wait another day to know the answers to questions she'd never wanted to ask. If only she didn't feel so alone in what had become one of the scariest periods of her life.

# *Chapter Five*

So much for off duty, Zach thought as he trudged through Winchester Park Monday afternoon, peering at community members huddled around picnic tables and reclining on blankets. If not for his German shepherd, Rudy, coming along to beg for picnic leftovers and sniff other pooches, Zach could have forgotten even pretending he was enjoying his day off at Chestnut Grove's community Labor Day picnic.

Even with his seventy-pound prop, this still felt like just another day at the office. He was too keyed up to even smile at the squeals of children playing on the wooden play structure and the crack of a base hit on the brand-new baseball diamond. Enjoying watching paddleboat races on the man-made lake or a game of horseshoes seemed impossible when he was busy studying all of his friends and neighbors with suspicion.

"Hold on, buddy," he told Rudy as the dog strained

against his leash. "They're not going to give you their lunch."

The dog only looked up at him and whined before pulling again.

Zach held tight on the leash until his "puppy" heeled. "You've got it easy. No worries. Just a bowl of kibble and a squirrel to chase, and you're good."

He, on the other hand, couldn't turn off the details of the case, even for enough time to enjoy some of the Starlight's locally famous fried chicken in his bachelor picnic lunch. Five days had passed since Gabriel had been discovered, and the department wasn't any closer to finding the infant's mother.

The situation was too serious for him to worry about betraying his friends by studying them as possible witnesses in his case. This was a small town. Baby Gabriel didn't just fall out of the sky to show up on Tiny Blessings' doorstep. Someone had to have seen something, had to know something. What he had to figure out was who wasn't telling and why.

*Lord, please lead me to the answers in this case. Show me the way to locate this child's mother. Amen.*

Obviously his skills for surreptitious observation while praying open-eyed were out of whack because the Frasers' oldest, Jonah, waved and shuffled over. The ex-marine's limp had either become less pronounced or Zach had just become used to it in the nine months since Jonah had returned to Chestnut Grove with a Purple Heart and an injury he'd never fully explained.

When he reached the dog, Jonah bent over to ruffle his fur but didn't crouch down. "How's our Rudy doin'?"

He stood to face Zach. "Hey, Detective, could we have picked a better day for a picnic?"

Zach gripped Jonah's hand, already roughened by a summer's worth of carpentry work. "Yes, this one came made to order."

"So now I know what Dad was praying for in his office last night."

Unconsciously, Jonah shifted his weight off his injured leg, making Zach wonder just how much pain the younger man was in. The side of Zach's mouth pulled up at the thought, though Jonah missed the expression as he watched Jared Kierney playing chase with his twins. Marines weren't exactly known for crying over little aches and pains. Or for their candidness about risky missions. Zach shrugged, reserving that mystery for another day.

"Is Ben keeping you busy at Cavanaugh Construction?"

"Can't complain."

The minister's son could probably complain about a lot of things over his life's newest detour, but Zach didn't mention it as Jonah waved and went in search of his family.

Continuing past a smattering of picnic tables, Zach scanned the crowd again. What was he looking for, really? Did he expect someone to stare straight at him and flash a sign that read, "I know something"? Some people were good at keeping their secrets, some better than others. And though secrets didn't necessarily beget secrets, they were at least a place to start.

He had to smile when the first people his gaze landed on were Beatrice and Charles Noble, who were pushing their adopted daughter, Gracie, in her stroller. Beatrice waved and pointed down at her toddler, whose eyes were wide with excitement. If that family wasn't an open book, then Zach wouldn't recognize one if he saw it.

The couple had gained a reputation as being a bit eccentric for Beatrice's vegan diet and macrobiotic cooking, and for Charles's penchant for wearing the family's Scottish kilt to special events, but the two were honest and caring. Besides founding the charitable Noble Foundation and raising their adult daughter, Rachel, who now ran it, they'd opened their hearts and home to Gracie, a child born with cerebral palsy but who was making amazing progress under their care.

He looked past the Noble family to the water where Miranda Jones and her lifejacket-clad son were laughing and turning their paddleboat in a circle. Now there was someone with a secret. At least she had been vague about her past and seemed to prefer to let people believe her life had begun two years before, when she'd appeared in Chestnut Grove. Again a mystery for another day.

Ben Cavanaugh caught his attention then, as the young widower kicked a soccer ball with his own adopted daughter, Olivia. Ben was a part of a secret, all right, but he was a reluctant participant in the intrigue and an even more reluctant witness.

When Zach had spoken to him about his own birth records being among the falsified documents found at Tiny Blessings, Ben had said he was all for letting sleeping dogs lie.

Unfortunately, Zach didn't have the luxury of being able to do that. But he also couldn't focus on that mystery, buried for thirty years, until he solved the one that had been around for just a few days and likely had a more critical deadline.

Finally giving up on his observation plan, Zach let Rudy drag him toward the main picnic structure, where families were staking out their spots. In the middle, on a colorful quilt, he saw the olive-skinned and black-haired family that he sensed he'd been looking for all along. Only the Estes family was one short, as Pilar wasn't with her parents, Rita and Salvador, and her brother, Ramon.

As soon as their gazes met, spry Rita popped up and waved him over. "Would you like to join us for some lunch, Zach? We have *pollo habichuelas colorados*."

"That's red beans with chicken. Red beans are a Puerto Rican specialty." Ramon offered only the translation instead of reinforcing his mother's invitation.

"Yes, please join us," soft-spoken Salvador chimed.

"That's very kind of you to offer, but I already have some of Isaac Tubman's fried chicken waiting for me."

Zach wasn't surprised by Ramon's closed-lipped smile over his decision. Pilar's older brother had never been unkind, but hadn't been especially friendly during the two years they'd attended church together.

Immigration attorneys and law enforcement officers didn't tend to mix well, so he never took Ramon's stand-offishness personally. Zach figured that was what it had to be since he'd never intentionally done anything to offend Ramon. Except being more preoccupied with the man's sister than was necessary for a witness in a case, his subconscious added without permission. He shook away the thought as unreasonable, both in its premise and in its implication.

But that dangerous part of him he'd never fully been able to control couldn't resist testing his theory concerning Ramon. "Have any of you seen Pilar? I need to ask her some more questions."

"So this is a working visit?" Ramon asked, his voice dripping sarcasm. "Can't the Chestnut Grove PD afford holiday pay for its detectives this year?"

Zach studied Ramon for a few seconds. With his dark good looks, he was a male version of his sister, but without her delicate cheekbones and dramatic eyes. Ramon resented him, all right, maybe just for the things he'd mentioned and possibly something more.

"Ramon!" Rita's tone was sharp, probably the same one she'd used to stop her children from squabbling. "Detective Fletcher, please, you must forgive my son. He is rude." But then she glanced over her son's shoulder, her agitation growing more pronounced. "Our daughter, she has not yet joined us."

"She'll be along anytime, Margarita." Salt-and-pepper-haired Salvador used the mediator's tone that must have worked well for him in the twenty-some years he'd owned Main Street Hardware.

"That child is always making her mother wait." Rita spoke of Pilar's mother as if she and that other woman weren't one and the same.

"But she is a good daughter."

Rita turned to her husband, a small smile pulling at her lips. "*Sí,* she is."

Ramon cleared his throat loudly. "Is this a love fest for my sister or a picnic? I don't know about the rest of you, but I'm starved."

Rita opened her mouth to apologize for her son a second time, but Zach waved off her comment.

"I have a few others I need to talk to. This is my day off, but it's also one of the best opportunities to question several community members at the same time."

He adjusted his grip on Rudy's leash and smiled at Ramon. "I'll check back with *you* later."

Disappointment trailed after him as he walked away from the Estes family, whether because Pilar hadn't been with them or because he hadn't been immune to Ramon's baiting, he wasn't sure. He'd never gotten used to people who saw police as a threat rather than as support. When their resentment no longer bugged him, it would be time to turn in his badge.

As Zach continued across the park, he gave up trying to convince himself he was still looking for clues.

He knew exactly who he was looking for. That he'd been unable to take his eyes off her at church on Sunday should have offered him a billboard-size clue.

What he would ask her when he found her, he had no idea. He was running out of questions on the case, especially since she continually dodged them. He had a fleeting thought that he should ask a different sort of question—such as, for example, if she was available for dinner—but he banished the idea. When was he going to get his mind off his nonexistent social life and focus on the case?

Instead of wondering about any breaks in her social calendar, he should have been wondering if her not being at the event was a clue about what she was hiding. More than that, he should have been seeing if there was anything he could learn from others absent from this not-to-be-missed social event.

Mayor Gerald Morrow and his wife, Lindsay, were the most notable absentees, but they might have just been away making a goodwill appearance. He made a mental note to check back issues of the local newspaper to see if Morrow had announced plans to attend any events this week or if he'd scheduled vacation.

Zach was concentrating so hard that he didn't realize anyone was following him until he felt a tug on his jacket sleeve. Ruth Fraser grinned up at him when he turned back to her.

"How's it going, Ruthie?"

"Better now that you're here."

Her hopeful expression pulled at his heartstrings. Crushes were serious business for a sixteen-year-old. Even someone as war-roughened as he was could remember softer times when tender feelings were involved. He certainly didn't want to hurt hers if he could help it.

He chuckled to lighten the conversation. "If I've improved it, this picnic must have been a nightmare before I got here. A real dud, eh?"

She rolled her eyes but smiled.

Just beyond her, he saw Meg Kierney, Rachel Noble and Anne Smith spreading a long checkered tablecloth across a picnic table. Chestnut Grove was too small a town for him not to know these were Pilar's closest friends. If she wasn't with her family and wasn't with her friends, where was she?

"Mom would complain about my manners again if I didn't ask," Ruth was saying when he tuned back into what she was saying.

"I'm sorry. Ask what?"

"Taking a mental siesta, Zach?" But her words came with a forgiving smile. "I asked if you wanted to share our picnic lunch. And I said Mom would complain about my manners again if I didn't invite you."

"You're right about that, but—"

"You know Mom makes enough for an army. She doesn't want anyone to go hungry."

"Right again, but I've already got more than enough for me. My cooler's in the car." He patted her shoulder, careful not to offer a personal touch that she or anyone else might mistake as flirtatious, and stepped back.

"Oh, that's too bad. I know she'll hate to see good food going to waste." At least Ruth had the decency to tilt her head down and look sheepishly out from behind her copper bangs. The word "good" and her mother's cooking wouldn't often be included in the same sentence.

"Thanks for the offer, anyway." With a wave, he turned and took two steps away from her.

His thoughts were already miles ahead of him. People didn't just miss the community's Labor Day celebration without an explanation, and he had an idea that he might need to hear Pilar's.

"I guess Pilar will just have to eat more then."

If he'd been turned into a pillar of salt like Lot's wife in the biblical story of Sodom and Gomorrah, he wouldn't have stopped in his tracks faster. His pulse stuttered, and his mouth went dry. Slowly, he turned back to the teenager, hoping it would look like an afterthought.

But Ruth's raised eyebrow and her tilted head said she wasn't buying it. He couldn't blame her. He wasn't fooling anyone, least of all himself, that his interest in Pilar Estes was merely professional.

"Hey, everybody, look what the cat dragged in," Ruth called out as she pulled Zach by the arm into the circle of lawn chairs where the Fraser family had made camp.

At least the teen, who was too smart for her own good, hadn't called him on his sudden decision to join the Fraser family after all. She'd even waited patiently while he'd stopped to get his own food.

Reverend Fraser set his plate aside and stood to greet Zach with a firm handshake. "Well, hello there. How's life at the police department?"

"Always busy."

"Same in my business. Somebody's always coming and going." The minister's hearty laughter filled the air, and soon several of those around him were joining in.

Zach wanted to say that his job involved more of life's often-violent departures than any arrivals, but he doubted anyone would laugh at that.

Over by the table, Naomi turned from a crockery pot of what had to be overcooked potato casserole and hurried over to hug him.

"So glad you could join us, Zach. We've got plenty to eat." With her hand, she gestured toward a picnic table full of food containers.

"Thanks. Ruth passed along the invitation. Sorry, I won't be more help with eating everything. I brought my own food." He lamely held up his small cooler.

"Eat with us anyway. We'll make sure that dog of yours has plenty of scraps. And maybe you'll be able to pry Gabriel from Pilar's hands for a few minutes." She indicated with her hand just past the circle of chairs where Pilar sat cross-legged on a blanket and was feeding the baby a bottle.

Her head popped up at the sound of her name, and she startled when she noticed Zach. Until that moment, she probably hadn't noticed anyone around her except for the child in her arms. Again he wondered why. Again he didn't figure she would tell him.

"Oh, hi, Zach," she said as she stood up and let Naomi take Gabriel from her.

He'd never seen her dressed so casually before, in jeans, a summer sweater and sandals. She'd even worn her hair long about her shoulders. When he started to wonder what it would feel like to touch the long strands, he banished the thought from his mind.

"Hi."

"Who do you have there with you?"

He patted the German shepherd on the side. "This is Rudy."

Pilar let him sniff her hand first and then scratched his ears. Rudy started licking her hand and strained against his leash when Zach pulled him back.

"I saw your family."

She jerked her head to look around. "Where were *Mami* and *Papi?*"

"Near the lake. Sounds as if your mother was expecting you."

She grinned. "That bad, huh?"

"Let's just say she's mildly annoyed."

"I'd better get over there then. *Mami* does like her schedule." With that, she turned and hurried across the grounds.

Zach couldn't help watching her as she went. Her answers still hadn't told him much, but what she had said had only created more questions in his mind. What was it about her that left him wanting to know more? Though she'd been aware her mother wouldn't appreciate her tardiness, she'd still been unable to resist the chance to spend time with the baby.

Naomi laid the sleeping infant in a portable crib next to the picnic table and came to stand next to him. "Too bad Pilar couldn't eat lunch with us. But then Salvador and Rita probably miss her."

With effort, he pulled his gaze back from Pilar's retreating form. "Why's that? They live nearby."

"Sweet Pilar has come visiting at our house every day since Gabriel arrived. Her lunch hours, after work. I'm getting used to having her around."

Naomi smiled at her revelation, but it only ate at Zach's consciousness. Gabriel. With Pilar, everything went back to Gabriel. What the connection was he hadn't figured out yet, but he sensed it to his bones.

From behind them, Reverend Fraser cleared his throat, causing both to turn back to him.

"Zach, I'd like to introduce you to one of our new friends." He gestured toward a man sitting in one of the chairs and balancing a plate of food on his knee. "This is Ross Van Zandt."

The man set his plate aside and stood to shake Zach's hand. Ross had dark hair and intense dark eyes, and, from the look of the stubble on his chin and upper lip, had misplaced his razor about three days before.

"Ross, this is Zach Fletcher, detective for the Chestnut Grove Police Department." The reverend glanced back to Zach. "Ross has only been in town a few days."

Zach's gut clenched. He'd just spent the last twenty minutes observing everyone he knew, looking for leads, and he'd overlooked a newcomer with an arrival date that nearly coincided with his investigation. Or at least the case he should have been working on if his investigative skills hadn't suddenly taken a Puerto Rican holiday. Did he need any bigger sign that he needed to march into the chief's office and hand over this case?

"Nice little town you've got here," the newcomer said as he gripped Zach's hand.

"We like it." Zach tied Rudy behind his seat and gave the dog his own plate. When he was satisfied that the dog didn't mind the food, he lowered into one of the chairs and opened his cooler.

"You've got a beautiful dog."

Zach glanced over at Rudy with affection. "He's my pal. Always happy to see me and never asks where I've been."

Instead of continuing to make small talk, Ross returned to his seat and picked up his plate. He took bites of some probably less-than-tasty baked beans, but his gaze flitted from one side of the park to the other.

Occasionally, he even tilted his head almost inconspicuously to the side to see what was going on behind him. Studying the perimeter. Knowing where the exits were and who was going through them. A cop? His firm-looking build made it a good guess, and his expression that gave nothing away made it a better one. All of these were things Zach should have noticed earlier, if he were only looking.

Naomi stepped over to hand the newcomer a cup of lemonade. "You never told us what brings you to town."

"Work," he responded noncommittally. "I'm here working on a case."

Until that moment the Frasers' foster daughter, Tori St. Claire, had been sitting next to Ross with her blond head resting in the cup of her palm, the epitome of teenage boredom, but now she came to life. "Really? Are you a lawyer? Or an FBI agent? Or somebody with the KGB?" Her voice shot up an octave with each question.

Zach stilled his facial muscles to keep from smiling. He had some questions himself, but he doubted he'd ask them with Tori's enthusiasm.

Ross appeared to be trying not to smile himself. "No, nothing like that. I'm a private investigator."

"Oooh, a private eye. A gumshoe. Just like *Columbo*."

He did chuckle at that. "I'm afraid it's not much like the TV shows. Mostly it's a lot of boring research and pulling needles out of haystacks."

Somehow Zach guessed whatever Ross was looking for in Chestnut Grove was far more interesting than sewing implements and piles of dried hay. Otherwise, why was he being so purposely vague?

Reverend Fraser glanced between the two men over the tops of his spectacles. "Well, looks like you've come to the right place. Zach, why don't you sit by Ross and answer some questions for him. If there's anything you can't answer, then Naomi and I have been around here a year or two—or thirty-five, so we'll give it a shot."

If ever Zach had questioned the insight of his mild-mannered minister, he would have to remind himself never to do it again. The man might have had the tendency to believe the best in people when they'd deserved nothing but the worst, but boy, could he read people.

He picked up his plate and cooler and stepped over to the other side of the circle. "I can do that—that is, if Tori doesn't mind trading seats."

The teen who'd gone from bored to starry-eyed in the last ten minutes over the man next to her, shrugged and gave up her seat. Ross glanced up at him with a guarded expression Zach would have recognized from the mirror.

He sat down and took a bite of his chicken before setting it aside. Reverend Fraser had one thing right: Some questions were about to be asked in the next few minutes. He'd just wrongly predicted who would be asking them.

# Chapter Six

"**W**hat can you tell me about a baby left on the doorstep of Tiny Blessings Adoption Agency last Wednesday?"

Ross jerked his attention up from his plate to the detective who'd just spoken in a hushed tone. "Excuse me?"

He studied the detective for a few seconds, waiting for him to explain the ridiculous question. Zach's face still held a mild expression, but his gaze was intense.

What a day Ross was having. First, he'd figured he'd really messed up when he'd accepted the Frasers' invitation to join them for lunch. Him with a minister's family—*that* was one for the record books. Now, when he finally figured he would make some headway by quizzing the very detective mentioned in the newspaper articles about the forged records, the cop was questioning him about another crime.

"I asked what you can tell me—"

He shook his head to stop him. "I heard what you asked, but why are you asking me? Do you think I'm the mother?"

Zach didn't even smile at the joke. Instead, he shrugged. "Was worth a shot."

From his experience as a New York City cop, Ross gathered that the detective had asked him point-blank to study his reaction, his body language.

"Sounds like a tough case."

"Getting tougher by the minute." Zach stared off into the distance for several seconds before whipping his head back to him. "How many years were you on the force?"

Ross noted with a grin that he hadn't asked *if* he'd been a cop, only when. "About eight years—until two years ago."

He braced himself for a question about why he'd left. How would he sidestep it this time? But Zach only picked up his plate and took a bite of that chicken that smelled far better than anything on his own plate. It shouldn't have surprised him that the detective hadn't delved into his personal life. The man was a cop himself. He had to know there were as many reasons to leave the force as there were reasons to stay.

But before Zach changed his mind and decided to ask, Ross jumped in. "Hey, I thought I was supposed to be the one asking questions."

A dimple appeared in Zach's cheek as the side of his mouth pulled up. "Ask away."

"Got any more of that chicken?"

Zach shot a glance at Naomi, who was busy talking to an attractive young woman with striped blond hair, and slipped him a crispy-looking chicken leg. He took a big bite and paused to appreciate it. "Where'd you get this stuff?"

"The Starlight Diner. Sandra Lange's place has the best chicken in town."

"I'll keep that in mind." Sandra was also his whole reason for being in town, but he didn't mention that. "This looks like a big event. Do all of the community officials make appearances here? Town council members? Police chief? Mayor?"

"Usually they do. I haven't seen Mayor Morrow around today, but he might have been away on business."

"That's probably it." Probably laying low like the snake he was, Ross figured, since the news of the forged birth records had come to light.

The honorable mayor, or *dis*honorable in this case, was also a major player in his investigation. If not for the philandering former prosecutor seducing and getting a young woman pregnant, and then stealing her baby, there wouldn't be a case at all.

"Got any other questions?" Zach prodded.

Plenty, but several that he couldn't ask right away, so he turned the subject back to the detective. "What's the story about the baby?"

Zach stiffened for a few seconds and blew out a frustrated breath. "We have a few leads about the mother, but nothing has panned out. That little guy is still without a mother." He indicated with his head toward the portable crib.

Ross choked on his swallow of lemonade. "That's *the* baby?"

Zach nodded, staring at the baby, his expression grim. "The Frasers are licensed foster parents."

"And the Hispanic woman you were talking to earlier. Who was she?"

"She's the Tiny Blessings employee who discovered the baby. I've questioned her a few times about the case."

Somehow Ross managed not to chuckle. He'd looked at women a few times the way Zach had been staring at the black-haired woman.

"I need to find the baby's mother, and soon." Zach shook his head and turned back to him. "But you were asking questions about your case."

"Like I said, I just do the boring stuff." Too bad he wasn't ready to talk about his case yet. Detective Fletcher could have been a valuable resource.

"Something tells me I wouldn't be bored with it."

Ross shrugged. "And some people have a high tolerance for boredom."

Zach smiled. He didn't believe him for a minute.

They were at an impasse, and both of them knew it. The only problem was one of them was a Chestnut Grove police detective who could make it plenty difficult for the other one to get the answers he needed. Ross's reticence had probably only piqued Zach's interest about what he was investigating, and it wouldn't do to have the police following him around, looking under every stone he turned over.

An olive branch was in order.

"Look, I don't want us to get off on the wrong foot. I'll just get the answers in my boring little investigation and be on my way."

Zach nodded. "If you come up with anything in your boring little investigation that you can't handle, you'll be in touch, right?" He pulled out his wallet and handed Ross his card.

"Will do."

"I could probably help you find some of the answers."

"I know you could, detective, but you've got a more critical case on your hands right now." Ross looked pointedly at the baby beginning to fuss in the crib.

Zach swallowed hard as he watched the baby, giving the clue that the detective was closer to this investigation than a professional distance required. Ross was almost sorry he'd played on the police officer's emotions to get what he wanted, but he had a job to do.

"You'll turn anything that gets too dangerous over to the authorities. Do I have your word?"

Ross flashed him a thumbs-up, and Zach shook his head. At least they both knew he was lying. He'd never shied away from danger, and he'd never accepted—or needed—help from anyone before, so he wasn't about to start now.

Mayor Gerald Morrow caught his wife looking at him suspiciously again as he lay on the sofa Monday evening, so he coughed into his hand and blew his nose for her benefit.

"You still don't look that sick to me," Lindsay sniffed in the hateful way she always spoke to him when no one was around. The acid barely burned anymore.

She sat stretched on the chaise lounge, looking like a bad waif-model wanna-be in crepe slacks, a silk sweater and open-toe Ferragamos. She would have worn the getup, purchased during one of her weekly jaunts into Richmond's most exclusive boutiques, to impress the crowd at the Labor Day picnic.

Would have, not had, since he'd shown up in his robe and slippers, claiming a fever that she could have ruled out if she'd touched him. Good thing for him she never touched him except during photo ops. She was also too worried about appearances to show up without him, so she'd stayed home, questioning whether he was really sick. Anyway, he was sick, just in a different way than he'd told her.

"I feel lousy, I told you." He coughed good and hard to prove it. "My head aches, my chest aches and my ears ache. Everyone will understand. The last thing I needed was to be out there in that wind just to give a five-minute welcoming speech."

Lindsay played with her black hair, but it only fell back into the perfect pageboy shape that she'd always worn. Her steely blue eyes trained on him, though.

"That welcoming speech was a perfect opportunity

for you to secure votes in the next election, and you're a fool if you don't court every single vote."

"You know as well as I do, I've had a great first term so far. Unless city council turns against me or Chestnut Grove faces a natural disaster, reelection should be a cakewalk."

Anxiety had him shoving his hand back through the hair that seemed to have turned white and receded overnight, just before his sixty-fifth birthday. He was more worried about a not-so-natural disaster of horrific proportions if the truth about him and Sandra Lange came to light.

"Unless," Lindsay repeated.

His intake of breath was so automatic that Gerald had to cough again to cover it. He carefully adjusted the blanket over his lap. Did his wife know anything? She couldn't. He'd covered his tracks so well. Only three people knew the truth: One was dead and the other two had kept mum. At least until now.

But Lindsay didn't point her finger at him and shout that he was an adulterer, so he let himself breathe again. He had no doubt if she ever found out, he'd find himself sitting in the middle of Main Street with nothing but the suitcase and the cheap suits he'd brought to his advantageous marriage.

His wife continued as if she didn't notice the heart attack she'd nearly given him. "Sitting back on your lazy laurels isn't going to get you a second term. How are you ever going to get me—*us*—into the governor's mansion before you die of old age if you can't even earn a second term here?"

How was he going to get them into the governor's mansion if he couldn't keep the skeleton in his closet quietly hanging in the back?

"I've stood beside you an awfully long time waiting for that inauguration. I've given up a lot for you. The least you could do is give me the Richmond mansion." She opened her hardcover book and popped her nose inside, a signal that their conversation was finished.

He lifted his newspaper and continued the pretense that was their marriage. She didn't even have to list the sacrifices she'd made anymore because he'd memorized them.

Lindsay Chastain Morrow of the Richmond Chastains had given up her chance to be the real First Lady by selecting the wrong ambitious politician to champion toward the White House. By her choice, she'd given up any additions to the family fortune, which had been accruing since the Belle Air, the Evelynton and the Shirley plantations were still just starter farms in Charles City. And she'd given up the chance to produce an heir by selecting what she considered an infertile sire. If she only knew.

With just one case of infidelity in nearly thirty-eight years of marriage to Lindsay, Gerald figured he should have earned a medal, instead of standing on the brink of professional ruin. Unfortunately, elected officials' personal indiscretions were no longer being handled with kid gloves as they had been in the past.

His only choice was to somehow convince Sandra to keep quiet about their age-old affair and the child resulting from it. Guilt that he thought he'd finally mastered through thirty-some years of practice reared its ugly head again.

He wasn't the ogre Sandra believed him to be. He'd even cared for her in his own way and had felt badly about the child she'd lost, and about the emergency hysterectomy that prevented her from having other children.

He couldn't go further than that, though. Had she really expected him to give up everything—his foursome at the golf club, the convertible that always got him to court on time and the contacts that would one day translate into campaign donations—for poor domesticity with her?

Sandra had to understand that some secrets were too important not to be kept—then and now. That couldn't change just because of her unfortunate health circumstances. Some secrets simply should be taken to the grave. He'd thought he'd made that perfectly clear to her before. Apparently, she was going to require more convincing.

Pilar couldn't remember feeling more alone than that Tuesday morning while she sat in the hospital waiting room. She couldn't seem to breathe deeply enough to relieve her tight lungs, and her heart beat at an unsure rhythm that patterned her thoughts.

The organs in her abdomen ached by turns to compete for her attention. The sharp pains on her left side seemed more intense and more frequent this morning, enough to bring tears to her eyes, but then everything this morning made her feel like crying. The pain itself was probably just her body's reaction to the stress. It didn't help that she'd just consumed more water in the last forty-five minutes than was necessary to sustain a small country, and all she could do was hold her bladder and wait.

*Lord, please let everything be okay,* she repeated again and again, though it felt wrong to pray now when she should have been entrusting her worries into God's capable hands all along. She felt like a disobedient child running to a parent only after the trouble she'd caused came chasing at her heels.

She'd been so afraid to tell them before, but now she wished her family and friends were there to support her, at least lifting her up in prayer. Everyone except Kelly expected her to be at work this morning, and even her boss hadn't pressed for information when Pilar had told her she needed to be away for a few days after Labor Day. Kelly, of anyone, knew how much she'd needed a break.

At least the office staff wouldn't be shorthanded in her absence. Phone calls from prospective adoptive parents, or from pregnant women considering adoption, had only been trickling in even before the child abandonment story hit the newspaper. She doubted the phone would ring this morning at all, except from panicked adoptive parents wondering whether their adoptions were legal. Kelly had planned to field those calls herself.

Pilar shifted in her chair as another pain, still sharper than before, shot through her left side. Just how long were the hospital personnel going to leave her sitting there, hurting and not knowing? She wished someone would call her name, but at the same time, she hoped they would skip her altogether. Then she could hold on to her blissful ignorance just a while longer.

She felt the pain again, this time so intense that it seemed to radiate from her midsection all the way to the insteps of her feet. Squeezing her eyes shut, she waited for it to deaden. Could all of this be in her head, just a product of an overactive imagination and a bit of medical information?

"Pilar Estes," the nurse in the doorway called. She wore a bright smile to go with her bright blue scrubs.

Pilar followed the nurse down a fluorescent-lit hallway to a room where she was asked to change into a cloth gown. Soon she rested on a table next to a television monitor. A cold, sticky jelly had been smeared over her abdomen. Other women probably had lain in this same position hundreds of times, getting ready for happy introductions to their unborn babies. She didn't even want to think about what the ultrasound would tell her.

"Miss Estes, I'm going to press this against your abdomen now, so we can take a look at what's going on inside," the ultrasound technician explained.

All Pilar could make out on the screen was a series of lights and shadows, with a black void where she could only guess a baby would grow. The technician gave nothing away with her expression, but took some measurements and typed in some notes. Finally the woman pulled her instrument away from Pilar's abdomen.

"Can you tell me if everything's all right?"

The technician shook her head. "I can't give test results. Those come only from your gynecologist. But if you'll wait here a moment, I'll give her a call."

## Chapter Seven

Pilar awoke with a start, but no matter how many times she blinked her eyes, a heavy cloud of fog kept her surroundings from coming into focus. Her head pounded, and her mouth tasted like bile. Where was she, and why couldn't she get this weight off her chest?

She wrestled whatever held her until a warm hand squeezed hers. "Everything's fine, Pilar. Do you know where you are?"

At first she shook her head, but then in pillowy layers, pieces of her memory settled back into place. The remaining pieces tumbled over each other as bright lights and the IV stand next to her bed came into focus.

A ruptured cyst. Emergency laparoscopic surgery. No answers. As Pilar jerked to lift her head and shoulders up from the bed, dizziness and nausea entwined to press her back against the mattress.

The nurse had just stepped away, but she rushed back to the bed. "Miss Estes, you need to lie down."

Pilar shook her head, though she didn't lift it off the pillow. "I need to talk to my doctor."

"I'm sure she'll be in as soon as—"

"I need to see her *now*." Even she could hear the panic in her voice.

The nurse patted her hand and left the room but returned a few minutes later along with Pilar's gynecologist.

"Can you tell me what you found?"

The pretty young doctor smiled, but her expression held a sadness that wasn't usually there. It was all Pilar could do not to say that whatever it was, she didn't really need to know.

"Pilar, you understood the complication when we went into surgery, right? With a ruptured ovarian cyst, we had to go and attempt to save the ovary. Unfortunately…"

Whatever the doctor said after that came out like a cell phone call in a thunderstorm—the static and the rain itself distorting the message. Torsion of the ovary, she'd called it. Something about the large cyst causing the ovary to twist to give it more room to grow. The blood supply to the ovary had been cut off. Whether she'd understood the medical explanation or not, she'd gotten the most important part: one of her ovaries had died and was gone now.

Somehow she managed to nod when the doctor reminded her that plenty of women with only one ovary became pregnant. And she shook her head when the nurse asked if they could call someone to be with her.

Finally, she was alone in her recovery area, enclosed by four curtains of white, turned yellow by the lowered lights. Numbness inside her seeped to her extremities, leaving her hands without the strength to even pull up her blanket. This was what it felt like on the day your dreams died. So cold. So final.

She wanted to cry, but what would it accomplish? Futile tears for a pointless cause. So she lay there, her eyes dry, rocking herself gently, uncertainty smothering all her hope.

Her eyes closed for what felt like only a few more seconds, but when she opened them again, the lights were bright. The nurse was above her, wrapping a machine-operated blood pressure cuff around her arm.

"Are you feeling better now?" she asked with a smile. She handed her a cup with pills and helped her take them, telling her it was for the discomfort.

"Just a little while longer to let the anesthesia wear off, and you'll be able to get dressed and go home."

"Home. Are you serious?"

"Sure. Your doctor plans to release you today."

"But I didn't know…"

The nurse stepped over to check Pilar's IV bag. "Even your surgery today, though an emergency, was still an outpatient procedure, barring complications."

If she hadn't been feeling everything before, she made up for it now. How was she supposed to go home like this? Could she even drive? Could she care for herself once she got there? The nurse was still talking when Pilar found her way back to the conversation.

"Now all you need to tell me is who I can call to bring you home from the hospital. You read, of course, in the paperwork regarding diagnostic laparoscopic surgery, that someone else would be required to drive you home."

She hadn't read it, of course. She'd barely been able to digest the idea of the ultrasound, so she'd only skimmed the material on laparoscopic procedures, hoping she wouldn't have to deal with that.

The nurse stood at the foot of her bed, a pen poised above her pad, a perplexed expression on her face.

"Can I wait until I'm released to call? My friend is very busy, and I don't want to bother her until I know for sure I'm being sent home. It's still going to be a few hours, isn't it?"

The nurse quirked her eyebrow and then nodded. "At least another hour." She studied Pilar suspiciously, probably the veteran of other cases where patients had kept too many secrets for their own good. "That's fine. We'll wait. But remember, we won't be able to release you until someone comes to drive you home."

Pilar thanked the nurse, who collected her chart and left the cubicle. One hour. What was she going to do? She had only sixty minutes not only to produce a driver but also to find a way to speak aloud words she'd mostly avoided repeating even in her thoughts. Only an hour to explain why she hadn't trusted her friends and family with the questions that had been tearing her apart.

Eventually, she would have to tell each of them. At

least now she could admit that she needed to surround herself with people who loved her. But that was in the next few days, a week max. Right now, she had only one question on her mind: Who would she tell first?

Zach followed the sound of two feminine voices down the corridor of Bon Secours Richmond Community Hospital. His heart tapped out a staccato beat that outpaced his steps on the floor. He didn't know what was wrong with Pilar, but he did know that finally, after a few well placed calls and a few favors that were tough to call in, given hospital privacy laws, he'd located her.

He didn't even understand why his search for her had quickly become frenzied. Yet he'd sensed something was wrong the moment he'd dropped by the Frasers' during Pilar's regular lunch hour and had not found her there.

After he'd spoken with Kelly Young at the adoption agency and had learned that Pilar had taken a few days vacation, he'd worried that Pilar's secrets had come to haunt her. When he'd tracked her to the Richmond hospital, he couldn't drive fast enough.

He hadn't even stopped to consider whether he was the person she needed to come to her aid. She needed someone, and that was enough for him.

The voices grew louder as he neared the surgery center waiting room. Pilar, crouched in a wheelchair, and a nurse in blue scrubs came into view. What had happened to her? Was she okay? The impulse to race into the room and to demand answers was so strong that he had to brace his hands on the door frame to prevent it. From the doorway, he could see her, but she couldn't see him.

The nurse crouched next to Pilar's wheelchair and gestured widely with her hands. "Now Miss Estes, I thought you understood that you cannot go home alone. You cannot be released until your ride arrives."

Pilar sat in the chair wringing her hands. With her hair pulled back like that, he could see how pale she looked. She pressed her fingertips against her forehead as if she was in pain. "I'm perfectly capable—"

"I'm sure you are, but you understand, it's hospital policy. Now please tell me whom I can call to come for you. There has to be someone."

"That's just it. There's…"

Though she let her words trail off, he couldn't help wondering if she'd almost said "no one." That was unacceptable. His sister had once had no one. He could never willingly allow another woman to be so alone.

Without taking time to think, Zach pushed through the door and approached the two women.

"Pilar, can you ever forgive me? I meant to get here earlier, but I got caught up in an important investigation, and I lost track of time."

Her eyes widened. He doubted he needed to mention that she'd been the focus of the investigation.

"Oh." The nurse looked back and forth between Pilar and Zach. "You didn't mention that your ride was late."

"No, I didn't." Pilar opened her mouth to say more,

but when she glanced at Zach, he shook his head. Finally, she clicked her jaw shut.

"Well, we can release you now."

A few minutes and a few signed papers later, Zach pulled his car to the drop-off area. The nurse crouched in front of the chair and released the footrests as he came around the car.

"Can you walk?" Somehow he managed not to sweep her into his arms and handle the situation before she had the chance to answer.

"I think so. They wouldn't let me try inside." She glanced back at the nurse who'd moved behind the chair. "I know. Hospital policy."

At least Pilar had kept her sense of humor during what must have been a difficult day. He might have thought she was okay if not for the hitch in her breath when he helped her into the car. After he'd closed the door and had come around to the driver's side, she still sat with her eyes pinched closed and her hand pressed over her belly.

*What is wrong?* So many questions bombarded his mind, and she wasn't offering any answers. Gall bladder surgery? The *C* word? No, he refused to believe it was cancer. When other, more personal, suspicions filtered in, he pushed them aside, as well. He wasn't here to judge her. He didn't need to know. She needed a friend, and it appeared he was all she had.

"Thanks for coming." Her voice cracked with emotion that had nothing to do with his chauffeur service.

"Glad to help." He put the car in Drive and crept out

of the parking lot, moving slowly over the speed bumps. "Did they give you anything for the pain?"

She nodded but stared out the window.

"Seems to be working."

The side of her mouth lifted, though her chuckle sounded more like a grunt. Again, she clutched her midsection.

"Sorry about that."

"That's okay. The new dose hasn't taken effect yet."

New dose? Zach was more sorry he hadn't started looking for Pilar earlier in the day because she'd obviously been in Recovery long enough to have a second dose. But he'd had no believable excuse for his presence in her office first thing that morning, so there was no way he could have known.

If only she'd called him earlier to ask for a ride. That idea was ridiculous, though. She never would have asked him. Until the last week she'd barely known him, and since then she'd only rested like a pinned monarch butterfly under his magnifying glass of suspicion. Why would she have asked anything of him?

The idea struck him then that though she had plenty of good friends and a supportive family, she hadn't asked any of them to go to the hospital, either. What had she been so afraid of?

For most of the short drive from Richmond to Chestnut Grove, they drove in a silence so loud that Zach had to put on the radio to drown it out. Okay, he'd found her. Now what was he supposed to do? She was in no shape for him to interrogate her again, and yet that was exactly what he was tempted to do. None of the questions he wanted to ask had to do with his investigation though.

They had just turned onto Main Street when Pilar spoke again. "How did you find me?"

"Process of elimination."

Out of his peripheral vision, he caught sight of her smiling. The medication must have begun to take effect. "Did you start at the morgues and work backward?"

"Something like that," he said, though the muscles in his stomach refused to unclench. She'd meant it as a joke to lighten the heavy mood, but it was so *not* funny. It had been bad enough finding her at the hospital.

"Why were you looking for me in the first place?"

She'd turned her head to watch him, and he felt unsteady under her gaze.

"Remember that case I've been working on?" That was certainly part of it. Whatever else it was, he couldn't explain it to himself, let alone her.

"Always working so hard."

*Or hardly working.* He sensed that the afternoon's mad search hadn't put him any closer to answers in the child abandonment case. Professionally speaking, he'd wasted another day, allowing the infant's mother to go even further into hiding. But since she'd just given him what amounted to a sturdy branch stretched over the river rapids of their conversation, he grasped it with gratitude. "That's me, workaholic Detective Fletcher."

"Do you need directions to my apartment?" But she shook her head, not waiting for his answer. "Oh. Right. The police report."

They both fell back into their earlier silence, but the atmosphere felt less tense. Zach guessed it was from relief. Was she as relieved that he wasn't asking about her condition as he was that she hadn't demanded to know why he'd hunted her down?

After only a few minutes, they pulled to the curb in front of the Walnut Street town house that had been converted into apartments. Taking in the aged brick and tall windows with ornate moldings, Zach wondered how proud Pilar was of her east-of-Main address. He'd seen her parents' modest but well-maintained home. This place, though, represented a step up for Miss Estes.

Were possessions and prestige important to her? He didn't know. She didn't drive a flashy car, and her clothes didn't have any four-digit price tags hanging out. Beyond that, he wasn't much of a judge. Pilar was the one who'd pointed out that though Gabriel was found with a cashmere blanket, he was wearing dime-store jammies. Okay, she knew about designer labels, but he still didn't know if they mattered to her. Or what did.

Though he'd asked her dozens of questions in the last few days, it was surprising just how little he knew about her. And disconcerting to realize he wanted to know more. *Drive away now,* his survival instinct demanded, though it wasn't feasible with her still in the car. But he did need to step away. He was too close to this investigation for more reasons than before.

When he glanced back at Pilar, she was studying him and looking perplexed. Her expression softened to a smile. "You don't know how hard this is for me to admit, but I don't think I can get out of the car by myself."

"Okay then, I won't tell anybody."

She looked so grateful that his heart squeezed. Did she hope he would keep her interesting vacation-day excursion to himself, as well? Whatever thoughts of fleeing he'd had before evaporated like the mist that had settled on his windshield.

He climbed out of the car and crossed to open her door. With a hand below her elbow, he helped her out of the car, but she staggered as soon as her feet touched the ground. Instinct took over, and before he realized what he was doing, Zach had lifted her into his arms. She was light and, at this moment, vulnerable.

His mind returned to the morning of Gabriel's discovery, when he'd wrapped his jacket around her shoulders. She'd handed it back, he remembered, showing how little she appreciated coddling. This time, though, only a gasp escaped her lips.

"Sorry."

"That's okay," she whispered.

"Where are your keys?"

"Purse."

He looked down to see a small handbag dangling

from her arm. At least he wasn't going to have to crouch down and retrieve her purse from the car. He hated to think how much doing something like that would hurt her. Now if he could only get her inside her apartment without maiming her. He dug his hand into her purse and was amazed to come out with a set of four keys, one with black rubber edging to signal it went to an ignition. He strained to lift the key chain high enough for her to see.

"The gold one."

He fumbled with the lock and flipped the key over before it connected. "Which apartment is yours?"

"Upstairs on the right."

He grunted. "Upstairs. Of course." The police officer in him was relieved she wasn't one of those naive young women who risked living in a first-floor apartment.

"You don't have to carry me."

Turning the knob, he pushed the door open with his foot. "Is that so? You think you can walk?" Inside, he let the door fall closed behind them. A set of narrow mahogany stairs had him pausing at the landing.

She chuckled until her breath hitched again. "I could crawl maybe."

"What kind of gentleman would I be if I made a lady crawl up the stairs?" Turning sideways, he began the long slow journey. His arms ached from their positioning. Clearly, he needed to get back into the gym.

"I wouldn't tell anybody."

"I'd know. You'd know." And it was awfully important to him right now that Pilar see him as a gentleman, especially since he was holding her keys up again to ask which went to her apartment.

"Silver one."

He looked. "There's two of those."

"Square top."

This one went in easily, and he turned the knob and pushed it open. The place was tiny, dollhouselike, but it didn't look like any apartment he'd ever seen. There were curtains instead of just blinds.

Not only were there a real sofa and side chair, but there were fancy color combinations of pillows arranged on them. The place had tables with a few doodads on them, and, even more unbelievably, framed prints on the wall. It didn't take much, of course, to amaze a guy like him, who still had boxes in his apartment from two years before. As for wall decor, he hadn't put up anything that didn't attach with tape.

"A little overwhelming, isn't it?"

Pilar was looking up at him when he finally looked down at her. "It's nice. Now all you need is a big dog like Rudy, and you'd have it made."

"It would be pretty tight quarters with a dog."

"Yeah, that's probably right."

"I like your dog, though."

"And he likes you." Someone else did, too, but he didn't mention that.

Still carrying her, he crossed to an open doorway. A bed, dresser and still more fluffy pillows were inside.

Zach swallowed hard. What was he supposed to do now? "Uh, where do you want to land?"

She followed his gaze to her bedroom and chewed her lip. "The couch is fine."

Relief flooded through him. "Yes, the couch."

He carried her to the sofa and bent to lower her. As he lay her head back, he reached behind her and tossed several pillows to the floor to make more room for her.

Once she was resting against a deep green pillow made out of what looked like corduroy material, she let her head loll to the side. For several seconds, she studied the pillows on the floor as if colors and textures were overstimulating her.

"I guess I overdid it with the pillows. I just like to decorate, mixing colors and textures."

"You're a really good decorator."

"Not really, but thanks for saying so."

Not that he would recognize a really bad one if said decorator wallpapered him to the wall. If he kept on like this, he probably would be telling her she was talented and incredible in the next breath.

At least she wasn't looking at him as if he were some alien invader. She wasn't paying attention to anything, as her eyes first fluttered a few times and then closed.

She needed the rest after whatever trauma she'd faced that day. He hadn't asked her about it, and she hadn't volunteered anything, but he could see that she'd been affected by whatever it was.

Zach reached over the back of the couch and pulled

a rainbow-colored afghan over her. Though she didn't even startle in her sleep, he couldn't help but continue watching her.

If she'd seemed vulnerable before, when he'd first seen her arguing her case with the nurse, then it was nothing compared to seeing her now in sleep. Her skin appeared so smooth that he stuffed his hand in his pocket to keep from brushing her cheek to test the theory.

With her face so relaxed, she appeared innocent, trusting. What was it about Pilar that made him wish he was a different man, the type who could trust people the way she did? If he could pinpoint it, then maybe he could set it aside and get back to his policy of helping people without getting too invested. She tempted him to chuck that policy, and he just couldn't allow that.

But he couldn't leave her here like that, either. Beyond her likely needing help to face whatever had sent her to the hospital, she didn't have anyone there to give her a decent meal. The least he could do was provide that.

Backing slowly away from her so as not to wake her, he retreated to the safety of her galley kitchen. Rummaging through her cabinets, he found a can of chicken soup and a saucepan. While the soup was warming on the stove, he located crackers in a different cabinet and a jar of applesauce in the refrigerator.

As he arranged the things he found on a tray from under the sink, he scanned the cut-glass canisters and fancy towels strategically arranged in the small space. She'd managed to make even this place, no bigger than a small walk-in closet, inviting. Instead of temporary lodging, she made the place seem like a real home.

He hated to think how long it had been since he'd felt at home anywhere. But he shook away the notion. He'd thought he'd given up wasting energy on things that couldn't be changed a long time ago.

Hoisting the tray, he crossed the ten steps that landed him back in the living area.

Pilar faced him, having hoisted herself in an almost seated position. Her ponytail was mussed from her nap. Curiosity etched her features.

"Oh, I thought I was going to have to wake you up to feed you."

"You're not going to feed me, are you? If you do, I might die from humiliation."

He shook his head. "I meant when I gave you your food."

"Thanks for clearing that up."

"Here." Zach set the tray on the coffee table and shifted another pillow behind her back so she could sit up higher.

"Comfortable?"

When she nodded, he laid the tray across her lap.

"Thanks for making me dinner." She bowed her head for a few seconds and then lifted a spoonful of soup to her lips. "I didn't realize how hungry I was. Aren't you hungry?"

Zach shrugged as he lowered into the side chair. He had no idea what he was, except for out of his element.

This was a virtual no-man's-land in his world of walls, and he didn't know what to do without the safety of his concrete barriers.

She was studying him again. He could feel her gaze on him even before he looked up to confirm it.

"Tell me, something, Zach." She paused a few seconds before continuing. "Why are you still here?"

# *Chapter Eight*

Pilar stared back at the man looking at her as if she'd just pulled a gun on him or something. Though she was as curious as ever, she wished she hadn't demanded answers.

Now he was probably going to leave her here alone, and that was the last thing she wanted.

In her best dreams, she'd pictured Zach at her apartment a time or two, but she'd always imagined him picking her up for a date or maybe sharing a dinner that she'd cooked. This was not at all what she'd had in mind, and yet it was nice, too.

If she hadn't already recognized Zach Fletcher's many good qualities before, she would have seen him in a new light today. A compassionate, caring light. Zach had always seemed to keep a polite distance, but he'd been different all afternoon.

Whether he planned on it or not, they'd crossed the line between acquaintance and friendship the moment he'd let her into his car. If not then, surely it had been when he'd hauled her into his arms and carried her up the stairs. She wondered if he felt as unsettled about the change as she did. Somehow she doubted it. Her feelings where he was concerned were confusing enough without him being so nice to her.

Zach playing nursemaid threatened to make her wish for all kinds of things that she had no business thinking about with anybody, at least not right now. But that didn't stop her from wanting him to stay, and from regretting that she'd given him any reason to leave.

"Why am I here?" he repeated her question. "Because nobody else appears to be here except you, and you were in too much pain to get yourself out of the car."

Again, she was sorry she'd asked, but for different reasons.

His confident smile had replaced the shocked expression from when she'd first asked the question, as if he'd just put a mask back in place to cover his emotions. What was he trying to hide?

"It would be pretty unheroic for me to leave you here without at least making sure you had something to eat, wouldn't it?"

That was it. Zach had a hero complex, and he saw her as a damsel in distress. Even she'd been glad to see him roaring into the hospital like a rumpled knight, minus his white horse. In his job as a cop, he probably found candidates auditioning for the damsel role all the time. It just happened to be her turn.

Pilar swallowed the disappointment she shouldn't have been feeling. "Well, you've done your good deed for the day, so…" She let her words trail off, still not able to tell him to leave, but giving him the opportunity anyway.

"I'm in no hurry."

What had she expected? That he would just give in and walk out the door without balking? She'd underestimated how deeply ingrained his need to play the hero was. She just couldn't bear the idea that he'd only stayed with her out of some misplaced sense of duty or, worse, he'd felt sorry for her.

She could handle his rejection, had even become good at it over the last few years whether he was aware of her interest or not. His pity, though, was too much to take.

"Look, I'm really going to be just fine…" she paused under his questioning gaze "…in a day or so."

His smile softened. "I don't doubt that. You're a strong woman. Just look how well you've handled all the incidents at your work lately."

She waited for a smirk to cross his face since he'd mentioned more than once her odd connection to Gabriel, but his expression remained mild.

"Well, thanks so much for everything. I really appreciate you bringing me home, but—"

He spread his hands wide to interrupt her. "You know, I'd really like to stay, at least for a while."

Her heart squeezed. He *wanted* to stay. Now that was a hard one to argue with, even if his reasons weren't the ones she might have chosen. Especially since she wanted him to stay, too. She must have hesitated too long because he tried again.

"Look, we'd be doing each other a favor. I would really like to bounce some ideas off you in the child abandonment case."

"I'm not sure I can help." She shrugged, but he held up a finger to ask her to wait a minute.

"And *you* need a little help in the kitchen. You'll have to take another painkiller for your headache after you see the mess I've left in there."

She chuckled and only shifted slightly at the pain in her abdomen. Though she doubted she would find more than a dirty pan in the sink, she had to give him credit for his argument. He was making it far too easy to say yes when she needed to say no, probably for both of their sakes. But then she'd never claimed to be strong, especially when it came to her interest in Zach.

"You want to trade your elbow grease in my filthy kitchen for only a few of my incredible insights?" She pressed her tongue in her cheek as she waited for his nod. His lips pulled tight, but he didn't laugh.

"If you're offering to be a slave, then I'm getting the better end of the deal."

Zach pressed a fist against his mouth as if in deep contemplation. "Maybe *slave* is too strong a word."

She couldn't help grinning. "Would you prefer domestic assistant?"

"If I have to."

"You have to."

Zach stood and bowed gallantly. "Zach Fletcher, domestic assistant, at your service."

"Then your first assignment is to scrounge something up for yourself. There's no way I'm going to eat alone."

Without an argument, he crossed to the kitchen and started banging around in the cupboards. In a few minutes, he returned with a plate containing two peanut-butter-and-jelly sandwiches and two pickles. Under his arm he carried two cans of lemon-lime soda, one of which he handed to her before taking a starving-man-size bite of his first sandwich.

"Try not to eat the stoneware, okay?"

He wiped jelly off his lip with a napkin. "Sorry. Long time between meals."

"Don't I know it." She took another bite of her soup. It was getting cold and didn't go down as easily as the first bite, but she tried not to let him notice. "Hey, you didn't offer me a PB and J."

"I didn't know if you'd be able to eat anything solid after anesthesia. You're barely able to get that soup down." He set his plate on the coffee table and stood to retrieve her tray. "Here, let me warm that up again."

"It's fine, really."

"Cool it with the *fine* business, okay? I didn't even have surgery today, and I would probably toss my cookies if I had to eat this stuff cold."

Pilar opened her mouth to say something and then shut it. He appeared to accept that as a "yes" and carried her tray back to the kitchen. When Zach returned a few minutes later, he'd placed half of a peanut-butter sandwich on the tray with the soup.

He indicated the sandwich with a nod as he lowered the tray back onto her lap. "If you can keep the soup down." He returned to his seat and picked up his sandwich again. "Are you still having much pain?"

"It's better now." The broth clogged her throat as Pilar braced herself for his questions. She didn't know how he'd managed to wait this long, how he'd avoided interrogating her even before he'd helped her out of the wheelchair and into his car.

But Zach only settled back in his seat, putting away the rest of the first sandwich in two big bites. He wasn't even staring at her the way he often had lately.

She took another bite, chewing slowing on the slippery noodles. Still, he didn't ask. Wasn't he even curious?

She couldn't take it anymore. "Well?"

"Well what?"

"When are you going to ask me why I was at the hospital?"

He lifted a shoulder and lowered it. "You'll tell me when you're ready. Or not."

The odd thing was he didn't seem to care which option she chose. He'd planned to stay to help her without insisting that she confide in him. His offer, unconditional like God's love, wrapped itself warmly around her heart.

Silence returned as they finished their food, but it was a companionable silence. Comfortable. Pilar didn't allow herself to wonder why the only time she'd felt comfortable in days was with someone as unlikely as Zach. She just let herself enjoy it.

"You said you wanted to bounce some theories off me?"

Zach set his plate aside. "I'm trying to toss out a few of the theories. Like the one about the blanket and the basket being from a break-in. I can't rule it out completely, but I ran a check on B and E's the last six months from here to Richmond, and I came up with zilch."

"Maybe those were just attic treasures that no one has noticed were missing yet."

He tilted his head as if considering. "Or maybe they weren't stolen at all."

"Then how did possible heirlooms get matched with Gabriel's dime-store-special clothes?"

"That's the big question. We found the exact sleeper and receiving blanket the baby was wearing at three different local discount stores. All the stores were part of national chains."

"So she could have come from anywhere?"

He shoved a hand back through his hair, his frustration palpable. "Information from area hospitals supports that theory. Only a few single women matching the mother's possible description gave birth around here."

"Well, that's something to go on."

"They've all checked out. Now we're looking at clinics all the way to Waynesboro."

"Could Gabriel have been a home birth?" But she

stopped and answered her own question. "Guess not. He was circumcised."

Zach nodded. "The doctors said his umbilical cord was professionally tied. If we don't find anything through clinics, we'll be hunting down licensed midwives next."

He looked so defeated that Pilar felt frustrated for him and ashamed that she'd hoped at the beginning he wouldn't locate the baby's mother. All of his leads appeared to be hitting brick walls, and she'd done nothing to help in his investigation.

Suddenly, she wanted to help him, even if his success meant an end to her secret hope of becoming Gabriel's mother. Even she realized it was an unrealistic dream. Right now, though, she wanted to do something to give Zach hope instead.

"What about the letter?" Her voice leaped an octave. "You thought it was a good lead, especially the paper."

His frown deepened. "As it turns out, that thick ecru stationery is expensive like we thought and not everyday stuff, but it's not as rare as we'd hoped for. Several nearby print shops either have it in stock or at least can order it. The handwriting analysis did confirm that the letter writer was probably younger than twenty, but that doesn't give us much to go on."

"It's still something, right?"

"It's not enough." He leaned his elbows on his knees and rested his head in his hands as he stared at the floor. "It's never enough."

As Pilar watched him, a strange awareness struck her

deep inside. She felt it as clearly as she felt those jabs of pain every time she shifted on the couch: The case was personal for Zach.

"Do you always take cases this personally?"

He didn't flinch or react physically to her question, but he didn't look at her, either. "Why do you ask?"

"I just get the sense that you're not telling me everything *you* know about this case."

Zach glanced at her, his head still cradled in his hands. "Funny question coming from you."

He didn't tell her more, and she had the feeling he didn't intend to, but she still couldn't help defending herself to him one more time. "I keep telling you I don't know anything about Gabriel's mother."

"And I believe you." His smile was halfhearted, but it was a start.

Who would have thought that such a small affirmation would make her feel so good? She was pitiful today. He hadn't said, "I believe in you," or anything of the sort, but he finally believed she was telling the truth, and that was enough.

"Who do you think she is, Zach?" She didn't have to tell him who she was talking about. His concern for Gabriel's mother was etched deeply between his eyebrows.

"Besides someone under twenty, I just don't know yet."

"Do you think it has anything to do with the altered records or the break-in at Tiny Blessings?"

He shook his head but appeared to be considering the idea. "I don't think so. The records were from so long ago. Barnaby Harcourt has been dead over a year now.

And the break-in appears to be about someone not wanting old secrets discovered."

"But Gabriel was right on Tiny Blessings' doorstep."

"It is an adoption agency. I don't think this incident is more closely related to the other two than that." He finished off his second sandwich, his frustration clear in the way he tore off bites.

When he was finished he scrambled to his feet and collected the dishes. "Want to know another thing I believe about this case?" he said over his shoulder. "Someone in town knows something."

Her shock must have been apparent because the side of his mouth came up when he turned to face her. "No, not you. But somebody."

"Do you think she's in danger?" she couldn't help asking.

"We'll never know until we find her, and if it takes too much longer to find her, if she is in trouble, we may be too late to help." His eyes were shiny, but he turned away and crossed to load the dishwasher.

How she ever could have thought him cold and distant, Pilar couldn't imagine. Obviously, he was deeply concerned about this woman, just as he'd been concerned for her when he'd discovered her missing. It went beyond heroics to someplace deep in his heart, and the truth of it couldn't help but touch hers.

Jared Kierney shifted in a visitor's chair at Tiny Blessings after regular office hours Tuesday, unaccustomed to feeling this nervous before an interview.

He'd been calmer interviewing presidential candidates stumping for votes than he was for this appointment. In fact, he would have preferred meeting with those officials, no matter how much rhetoric they spewed, than waiting here for Kelly Young, someone he and Meg had always considered a friend.

Did she still think of him in such kindly terms? He wouldn't blame her if she didn't. Would she understand that he was just doing his job when he'd reported on the information Florence Villi leaked to him? Would she believe him if he told her he would rather have done anything than to report past illegal activity at the agency that had brought him and Meg their precious twin sons? He'd prayed for her forgiveness a few times, but he'd never asked her for it.

As her friend, he should have tried harder to convince her it was a mistake to refuse comment when he'd first broken the story. He should have explained that to the public, a decision to decline comment pending an internal investigation was a red flag to demand answers.

Readers had demanded, all right, in letters to the editor and calls to the agency's office. If only she'd accepted his follow-up requests for an interview sooner. Then it would have been before the fire, before the discovery of the abandoned baby. Now the article he would write had gone from simple damage control to an SOS for a sinking ship. But he wouldn't let it go down, not if there was anything he could do, editorially, to help.

Jared shifted in his seat and tapped his index finger on the arm of the chair. What is taking her so long? He scanned her office for the twentieth time. It had no photos, no cozy accents. It was pin neat and all-business, like Kelly herself.

Through the doorway, a photo collage of happy, smiling adoptive families blanketed the wall. He knew all about those photos; his family was up there, too. God had blessed his family through this agency. He hoped it could survive so God could continue to use it to bless other families.

"Sorry I made you wait, Jared," Kelly said as she hurried into the office. "I was meeting with a few of our adoptive parents."

"No problem. I was so glad that Pilar told Meg you'd agreed to meet with me."

She smiled wanly. "I'd planned to call you myself."

"This way worked, too. Hey, I meant to say hello to Pilar when I came through, but she wasn't at her desk."

"She took a few days off."

He nodded, guessing why. Kelly could probably have used a few days off herself, but she didn't have that luxury as the boss.

"So…" He paused to gather his thoughts. "We can either begin with your prepared statement, or I can start from my list of questions. But before we begin, I want to remind you that there is no such thing as 'off the record.' If there is something that you want to tell me that is not for publication, please don't tell me, so there will be no misunderstandings."

"Thanks for saying that, but I'm not looking for any special favors just because your family has a history with the agency."

Jared swallowed, her shot striking its intended mark. "I'm sorry about the other article, but—"

"It's your job. I get that. But I would like to counteract some of that…unfortunate publicity with a positive article."

Great. He should have seen this one coming. She still wasn't going to answer his questions, but she wanted him to write a fluff piece anyway. Next thing he knew, she would be suggesting that he publish a grip-and-grin with her posing beside the latest big donor.

His skepticism must have been obvious because she raised her hand to stop whatever he'd been about to answer.

"Look, I know I'm not in any position to make requests, but hear me out first, okay?"

Jared lowered his spiral-topped reporter's notebook, leaned back in the chair and crossed his arms.

"I'll tell you everything I can. Remember, this is an ongoing investigation, so there are things Detective Fletcher has told me not to talk about."

He uncrossed his arms and took hold of the notebook again. "I wouldn't expect you to jeopardize the investigation, Kelly."

"I know." She paused as if weighing out whatever favor she was about to ask of him. But pride must have fought a losing battle with need because she leaned forward and pressed her hands on her desk.

"What about along with whatever news article you're planning, you do some feature profiles about some of our adoptive families, particularly some of our first families? We just celebrated our thirty-fifth anniversary in July, you know."

"I was at the party, remember?"

She nodded and paused again, probably waiting for him to really remember. Not that he could ever forget. If not for the anniversary party, he and Meg might never have realized they'd adopted identical twin boys who'd accidentally been separated. They probably never would have chosen to marry for their sons' sakes. Maybe they never would have fallen in love.

"Then you know how many great success stories Tiny Blessings has to tell."

"Sure. Meg and I have a pair of them." He didn't bother pointing out that their sons' adoption mix-up wasn't exactly a success in the beginning, since he figured God had a hand in how well it had turned out. "So what are you trying to say?"

"The falsified records are a horrible thing. You and I agree on that. A crime that shouldn't have gone unpunished if Barnaby Harcourt were still around to be held accountable. But neither should all of the families that

Tiny Blessings has helped to establish be punished for Barnaby's greed."

She had a point. Tiny Blessings had come under scrutiny, both legally and financially, since he'd brought the records' discrepancies into the public forum. None of the agency's former clients were immune, at least to the ripples from the scandal. In many ways, it wasn't fair. For every adoption record that was now in question, a few hundred happy families worried their adoptions would be legally challenged. What harm would it be for him to feature a few of them?

"A series of articles might be nice."

"Don't push it." But the sides of his mouth were already turning up. It was a good idea for some good news features. Jared liked to tell happy stories as much as the next reporter. He'd never bought into the newspaper credo that "if it bleeds, it leads," but he couldn't turn his back on important stories facing his readers, either.

"So, Jared, what do you say?"

He shrugged. "Get me a list of families who might agree to be profiled. It would be good if the families have adopted at different times throughout the agency's existence. After that, I'll see what I can do."

She settled back in her chair, seeming satisfied.

"Okay, ready?"

She straightened, but nodded.

"Have there been any new developments in the arson investigation regarding the duplicate birth records?"

"Not since your last update from the police department."

Kelly was no longer animated, but was stiff and robotic as she answered. He probably wouldn't get a single decent quote from her for this article.

He tried again. "After the fire, police reported that only a few of the duplicate records had been recovered. Were there any additional records recovered during the cleanup?"

"No. Most were destroyed in the fire."

How could she respond so calmly when, for some men and women given up for adoption more than thirty years ago, a last avenue for answers about their birth parents had been destroyed? What if it had happened to Luke and Chance? If they came to him with questions one day about their birth parents, could he tell them so dispassionately that their answers had gone up in smoke?

"What about your own adoption records?" As soon as the words were out of his mouth, Jared was sorry he'd asked the question that hadn't even been on his written list. Trying to shock her out of her remoteness wasn't a good enough reason.

She didn't move. To an outsider, she still would have appeared to be the same unflappable businesswoman who'd weathered this crisis. But he knew her better than that, and he'd never seen her so pale.

Didn't she realize he knew? Didn't she realize that Florence Villi had filled him in on several bits of information that he hadn't been able find a second source to confirm? Without a second source, he wouldn't publish anything.

"Yes, my personal records were destroyed." Again, she sounded distant.

"But it wouldn't matter anyway. I have no interest in locating my birth parents. I am the child of Marcus and Carol Young, and that's it. And that is most certainly *on* the record." She met his gaze steadily as she put extra emphasis on the word "on."

"Sorry about that. I had to ask."

She nodded blandly, but she had to recognize just as he did that he hadn't had to ask. He just had.

Whether she realized she'd just given him the second, confirming source to the information, she didn't seem to care. Now he had to grapple with his conscience on whether to use what he could now confirm. Was it newsworthy? Did it add depth to the article, or was it just a painful personal aside to a story with no happy endings? A more rabid reporter would have asked the follow-up question—if Ben Cavanaugh's records also had been destroyed—but Jared just couldn't bring himself to do it.

Most of the time he loved writing the news, being in the know, making sure everyone else got to be there with him. But then there were times when people got hurt because of some of the things he had to write, and on those days, he hated the job. This was one of those days.

# Chapter Nine

Pilar couldn't believe they'd been sitting there talking about nothing for the last two hours. She would never have guessed that much time had passed had the wall clock not announced the time with seven clear pings.

Their conversation had started when Zach had returned from the kitchen after he'd tried to hide how personally he was taking the case. Pilar had purposely not brought up the subject again. It wouldn't have helped anyway. They'd already discussed all the same leads he'd been following and had hit all the same walls he'd hit.

Instead, she'd mentioned Reverend Fraser's recent sermon on the story in the Book of Luke about the two thieves crucified alongside Jesus. Their conversation had taken off from there, and, aside from an occasional break to draw breath, they'd talked nonstop ever since.

She couldn't help grinning as she remembered Zach's confession that with his police background, he'd

had problems with that gospel story. He'd really strug-
gled with Jesus' promise to one thief—*Truly, I say to
you, today you will be with me in Paradise.*

"What are you smiling about?"

She chuckled at having been caught. "The thief
thing."

"That's the last time I confess anything to you."

He was probably joking, and yet she hoped it
wouldn't be the last time, either for silly things he would
confide in her or time they would spend together, just
talking.

She couldn't remember having felt more at ease with
anyone in a long time. Twice in the past two hours,
she'd momentarily forgotten why they were there, but
then she'd shifted positions, experienced the discomfort,
and it had all come rushing back.

Pilar cleared her throat. "Do you really want to know?"

He turned his head back to her, twisting in his strange
position in the overstuffed chair, with his legs dangling
uncomfortably over one of the arms.

"Know what?"

She didn't bother to reply, "You know what," since
they both knew what she was talking about.

"I only went in for an ultrasound this morning."

She waited for shock or some other reaction to reg-
ister on his face, but he only continued watching her.
"Looks like you got more than you bargained for."

His gaze lowered briefly to the light blanket he'd
brought her earlier to lay across her lap, and then he

met her gaze again. He was curious, sure, but never demanding.

The realization came upon her quickly, like a drizzle that transforms into a downpour, but Pilar suddenly wanted Zach to know about her. She needed someone to know, to understand what had been tearing her apart.

"It started with some unusual cramping."

Zach nodded, apparently comfortable discussing the intricacies of a woman's body.

"The doctor said there were cysts on my ovaries. Both. But one was larger. The ultrasound was to confirm her theory that I might have this condition that sometimes leaves women…infertile."

She stopped, the last word tasting of bile as she'd finally spoken it aloud. Glancing at Zach, she waited. What was she waiting for him to do, run away in shock? He didn't. He only continued resting with his head turned her way and waiting for her to tell him more.

Could she, when the story started at the bottom and only got worse from there? She gripped her hands together and forced the words from her mouth. "This morning the cramping became worse. Something wasn't right. I knew it wasn't right, but I wanted to believe it was only anxiety."

She knew she should slow down, but once the dam opened, she couldn't stop the story from pouring out. "The ultrasound showed the cyst had ruptured, so they rushed me into surgery. When I awoke, they told me my ovary had twisted and died. It's…gone."

The last came out as a sob that sounded as if it had come from someone else. When had she started crying? She couldn't recall a single tear, and yet her face was wet. And when had Zach moved from the chair to the edge of the couch by her? She didn't know that, either, but there he was, pulling the whole crying mess of her into his arms.

She didn't care that his movement brought sharp pains to the tiny incisions that marked a void inside her. She just let him wrap her in that cocoon of warmth and let all of the weight she'd been carrying fall where it would.

"I would have told…somebody…but I didn't…know… for sure," she managed to get out in an unsteady breath.

"Of course not," Zach crooned as he lowered her to the pillow and brushed damp strands of hair away from her face. His fingertips were cool against her hot skin.

"I just didn't want to…" Pilar let her words fall away, no longer certain what she'd wanted or why she'd thought it made sense. Nothing made sense now except Zach's comforting touch as he stroked her hair. Her hands gripped the sides of his shirt, and she couldn't let go.

"You didn't want to worry anybody."

Zach didn't even say it as a question as he finished for her. Did he really understand? How could he understand, when the secret she'd kept had ultimately left her alone on the worst morning of her life?

But she wasn't alone now, hadn't been since the moment he'd walked into the waiting room and had given her a no-strings offer of friendship. She felt undeserving of his offer, and yet she couldn't let him go now.

"I may never be able to have babies."

Zach's breath hitched in his throat. He inhaled slowly to calm himself, but all he wanted to do was curl up on the couch and cry with her, mourn with her. He knew what loss felt like. He could easily share that with her. But she didn't need his tears right now; she needed his strength. Leaning down and drawing her carefully into his arms again, he winced at her hiss of pain.

"I know. I know." But he didn't know, really, what she was going through, wondering if her dreams had slipped away while she'd been under anesthesia. He rocked her, wanting her to understand that though he didn't know, he still cared.

He pulled away and looked into her red-rimmed eyes. "How long have you been carrying this around inside you?"

"I went to the doctor Tuesday afternoon."

*And found Gabriel Wednesday morning,* his subconscious filled in for him. It all made sense now. Pilar had connected to this baby, not because of something she knew about him or his mother but because of the upheaval in her own life.

Timing had made the difference. A baby had arrived, like a heavenly gift, just as Pilar had been hit with the possibility that she would never have any. No wonder she'd been reluctant to help him locate Gabriel's mother.

"It's funny," Pilar said, though her voice held no

laughter. "It doesn't matter whether the doctor's diagnosis was correct or not. I only have one ovary left, and it's already got a cyst on it."

Her voice sounded as if she'd already given up hope, and he hated seeing her without it. He wanted to tell her that though he was no expert, even he was pretty sure that women with one ovary could still conceive. She probably wasn't ready to hear that. Maybe she needed to accept the worst-case scenario first before she could find her way back to hope again.

Strange, when she'd first mentioned the ultrasound, he'd immediately guessed she was pregnant. He didn't even want to think about how jealous the thought had made him. And Pilar probably wouldn't find the irony of his assumption all that amusing.

Pilar ineffectually wiped her tears and wouldn't meet his gaze, as if she'd only now realized all she'd told him and was sorry she had. He didn't want her to be sorry.

"Your secret is safe with me." Unable to resist, he brushed a glistening droplet from her cheek. She didn't turn away from his touch but pressed her cheek against his palm.

"Thanks. I don't know what I'm going to do about it."

"Praying would be a good start."

Her chest heaved as if she was about to start sobbing again, but she only stared at the floor. "How can I ask Him for help now, when I wasn't relying on Him all along?"

"What do you mean?"

When she looked up at him, a sad smile covered her lips. "Until this week, I'd never questioned God's will before, and for the last week I've done nothing but question."

He chuckled, and her eyes went wide. "Then you're a better Christian than I am. I question all the time." He shrugged and grinned. "But sooner or later He brings me around."

When Pilar nodded, Zach figured the Father would have a far easier time bringing her back to His will than He'd had with him. Though she was questioning, he wished he had even a small portion of her faith. But Jesus had promised that someone with faith the size of a mustard seed could move mountains. So even guys like Zach had a chance of being used for His will.

"It's just that everything's different now," she explained. "I was waiting patiently for God's time, but I always knew in my heart I would be a wife and mother someday. But now... How can I tell my future husband that maybe I can't...?" She let her words trail off as if they overwhelmed her too much to speak them aloud.

"You don't even know for sure you can't have children. It shouldn't matter anyway."

She just shook her head. "Already, I'm twenty-eight years old. Now I'm quite possibly infertile. Not the best recommendation."

What was she saying? While Pilar didn't say anything more, Zach suddenly had so many thoughts that he couldn't decide which to put into words first. Did she worry that no one would want her? That she was damaged goods? He couldn't bear thinking she thought of herself as substandard, for this or any other reason, for a man to choose her as his wife.

Didn't she know how beautiful she was? How clever? How kind? Didn't she realize that her goodness, her faith, gave everyone around her hope that they would find their way, as well?

"Some man is going to thank God for His blessings when he finds you."

Zach jerked, surprised that he'd spoken the words aloud. What had happened to his control over his emotions and his reactions? When he met her gaze, Pilar looked back at him with wide eyes.

He tilted his head to the side. "You know what I mean. Nothing else will matter then."

Her skeptical expression showed she disagreed with his conclusion, but she didn't call him on it. "Thanks for saying that." She paused and watched her gripped hands once more. "And thanks for today. You've been a good friend to me."

He smiled. Friends. Is that what they were now? So why did a seed of disappointment sprout inside him even though he'd convinced himself his heart was inhospitable soil? It was just another confirmation that he should never have taken this case in the first place. His good sense had plummeted the moment he'd told Sergeant Hollowell he could handle the case, and it only had gone downhill from there.

But this wasn't about what he needed. It was about

Pilar. And no matter what it had cost him, he was glad he'd been able to be there for her.

"It wasn't a huge trial, I guess." He chuckled for a few seconds and then steadied himself for what he needed to say next. What had to be said. "I've told you I won't tell anyone about your surgery, and I won't. But don't you think it's about time *you* did?"

Pilar winced. "I know I should, but—"

"At least your parents. Not that I know too much about close parent-child relationships, but don't you think they'll be sad they couldn't help their little girl when she was hurting?"

He was pouring it on thick, and he knew it. He'd done an awful lot of hurting without his folks around and had turned out just fine, thank you. But Pilar's family was different. They really seemed to care about each other. He could tell his comment had reached its mark the moment Pilar's lip started to quiver.

"*Mami* will never understand why I couldn't tell her."

"Maybe not, but Rita will still want to know now. She'll want to help." He cleared his throat, awkwardness filling it. "Besides, it's getting late. One of us really shouldn't be left alone tonight, and the other one…" he paused as he watched her fidgeting "…well, he wouldn't be a good choice to stay."

The minute she went from near tears to a grin of embarrassment, he knew he'd won. But he couldn't revel in his victory when she'd given up so much. Without saying more, he grabbed the portable phone from the kitchen wall and handed it to her. She didn't look at him as she dialed.

"*Mami,*" she said into the receiver with a quavery voice. She spoke in a rush of Spanish then, sounding so different from the woman he'd come to know. From his high school Spanish, he recognized the words *"lo siento"*—"I'm sorry"—though he would have guessed her meaning from her anguished expression anyway.

He felt like an uninvited observer behind an interrogation room's two-way glass, so he gave Pilar as much privacy as he could in tight quarters, heading into the bathroom and closing the door. No matter what was being said between the two women, he felt certain Pilar was in good hands now.

He was surprised, though, by his reluctance to turn over the job of caring for her to anyone else. Even her mother. He'd liked being the one she relied on. He'd liked being needed.

His reasons for staying were the same ones that shouted he should go. He was starting to care about Pilar too much. And caring before had only hurt him.

He needed to step away, take a breath, get some perspective. Tomorrow would be better. Tomorrow he would be back to his normal dispassionate self, and all would be well. It would even be all right, no more than neighborly really, for him to check back in on Pilar tomorrow. He would have the distance by then to be the friend she needed. At least that was what he wanted to believe. He had a sinking suspicion, though, that nothing could help him distance himself from Pilar Estes.

\* \* \*

Pilar stepped gingerly through her apartment's open slider to her balcony, and into Wednesday's late afternoon sun. More than twenty-four hours since her surgery, she was still sore, but she hadn't felt any sharp pains in at least an hour. That was progress.

The sun's warmth dancing on her skin and the deck's roughened wood beneath her feet made her smile. That tiny balcony that peeked out at Walnut Street had been her apartment's best selling point, probably its only selling point, when she'd moved in four years before, just after a February snowstorm. Yet she'd seen potential in the tight space, at the time buried beneath a snowdrift, just as she'd been able to envision a home inside the cramped rooms of the apartment itself.

Now a glass table was nestled between two muted-pattern deck chairs, and a flower box with still-blooming begonias shot their fuchsia color against the fading stained wood.

Rita Estes glanced up from one of the chairs where she was balancing a study guide across her knees. Her well-worn Bible rested near the chair leg.

"Good for you, *querida*. You are moving around well now."

"*Gracias, Mami.* I feel better." Pilar lowered herself into the other chair.

Rita stared down at Pilar's feet and frowned.

"You shouldn't be out here in bare feet. You'll catch a cold."

"I'll be fine. Besides, it's warm out today." She didn't even bother arguing about whether someone could catch a cold from being cold. At least some things stayed the same.

"It is good to get some food in you. I must start dinner." Rita collected her Bible-study materials and lifted out of the chair.

Good old *Mami*. She believed every problem could be solved with a big bowl of *caldo de pollo*. If only all solutions could be found while sipping her chicken soup.

Pilar touched her mother's arm. "Dinner can wait a few more minutes. Sit with me awhile. Please."

Rita glanced anxiously toward the kitchen. Schedules were important to her. Finally, though, she sat again. "A few minutes."

"Thanks for coming last night."

"You needed only ask."

Pilar tried to ignore her mother's lifted eyebrow and her unspoken censure. *Mami* still hadn't quite forgiven her for not coming to her first with her problems. Meg, Rachel and Anne would probably be angry when she told them, too, but she at least had a few days before she had to face them at Sunday brunch.

As it was, her mother's disappointment was enough to handle for one day. Though Rita had been caring for her with the same gentleness she'd always used when Pilar was sick, her hurt feelings were evident in things she'd said and in those she didn't say. All afternoon

Rita had been referring to Zach as "the detective" although she knew his name perfectly well.

Her mother's frustration was understandable. She probably didn't want to face that Pilar wasn't her little girl anymore. Did she feel betrayed because her daughter had confided in someone she barely knew instead of her? She had to understand, though, that sharing with Zach had been easier *because* they hadn't been close, not despite it.

Was that really the reason? She had to wonder. Maybe at first she could have said it was easier to tell him since they were only acquaintances and weren't invested in each other's lives. If that were true, though, now that they'd become friends, she would no longer want to talk to him, and she'd been thinking about doing just that for hours.

"How did the detective know you were at the hospital?" Rita asked the question as if they'd been discussing the surgery all day instead of dancing around the topic with the grace of prima ballerinas.

Pilar shifted in her seat. "He said he was looking for me and asked around."

Rita studied her daughter with the same direct gaze she'd used on Pilar whenever she'd been misbehaving. "He looked for you much lately. At the picnic also."

Pilar nodded, not sure what to say to that. For whatever reason, Zach had been looking for her, and now she was glad he had. If not for him, she might have still been in the hospital, still stubbornly avoiding contacting the people who loved her most.

She was too busy trying to wrap her own thoughts around the answer to her mother's question to notice more than a blur of color from a car passing on the street below them. But a door slam drew her attention to the road. The subject of her mother's question had just shown up to answer it himself.

# Chapter Ten

"Look, *Mami*, Zach has come to visit."

Pilar tried to speak calmly, but her voice sounded strained. She hoped her mother hadn't noticed. Already she was having enough trouble ignoring the nervous flutter in her midsection that had nothing to do with recent surgery. She didn't need her mother's questions to contribute to it.

"This I see" was Rita's only response.

Zach waved at them and then reached back into the car, emerging again with two large white carryout bags. Crossing the street, he came to a stop in the front yard, just beneath the balcony.

Holding up the bags, he indicated one with a tip of his head. "I didn't want to be presumptuous, but I thought you might be getting hungry, so I brought dinner."

Out of her peripheral vision, Pilar caught sight of her mother and waited. Would *Mami* again react with jealousy that Zach had encroached on her territory—that of her youngest child? But Rita's startled expression softened to a smile.

"So gracious from you, Zach. Come to the door, and I will buzz it for you."

Pilar didn't miss that her mother had used Zach's given name instead of referring to him by his job title. She quirked an eyebrow, but her mother didn't look back at her to catch her unspoken question about what had changed. At least she could relax now, knowing she wouldn't have to smooth any tension between her mother and her friend.

"Come to eat, *querida*," Rita called from inside the apartment a few minutes later. "Your *novio* has brought us Chinese."

Her *novio?* Pilar jerked as she came out of the seat and squeezed her eyes shut at the quick stab of pain. Her cheeks and neck burned for entirely different reasons. Why had her mother referred to Zach as her anything, let alone *novio,* a term that could just as easily be translated "bridegroom" as "boyfriend"? *Lord, please don't let Zach have a good command of Spanish.*

When she crossed through the slider, Rita was watching her, a strange, knowing expression on her face. Was she intentionally trying to embarrass her? If so, she was doing a great job of it.

Pilar sneaked a glance at Zach. Either he hadn't understood the Spanish or he'd been too busy unloading little white cartons to notice, but he finished what he was doing at the small dinette before he even looked up. Relief flooding her mind, Pilar glanced at her mother again. Rita only smiled.

"Zach, thank you." Pilar paused as she took her time getting into the dinette chair. "This was so nice of you."

"You'll join us, *sí?*" Rita asked, already setting three place settings on the table.

"If you think there'll be enough." There was laughter behind his smile as he scanned the collection of boxes.

"For Salvador and Ramon, as well, I think."

Zach chuckled as he took a seat between Pilar and her mother. "I guess I did overdo it. I'm used to ordering just for one."

Though the aromas of Mongolian beef, sweet-and-sour pork and cashew chicken were enough to make her mouth water, Pilar couldn't focus on food when what he'd said kept filtering through her mind. Ordering for one. She couldn't even imagine what that was like. Though she lived in her own apartment, with only a few calls, she could have the place crammed with friends and family.

What was it like for Zach having no relatives around to drop by too early on Saturday mornings and to remind him not to go out with wet hair? As much as she sometimes felt smothered by all that caring, she appreciated her support system.

Did Zach even have a system of people who cared about him? Did his family stay in close contact even if they didn't live nearby? Sure, he probably had friends at the police department, but she wondered if his apartment stayed empty even when he was sick of aloneness.

It wasn't until Zach cleared his throat that Pilar realized she'd been staring into an open container of white rice, her thoughts not so much on the dinner but on her fellow diner. "Oh. Sorry."

"Did I choose wrong?" He pointed to the food. "Maybe I should have brought the menu by."

"No, you picked fine." She busied herself by tucking a stray strand from her braid behind her ear. "I was just trying to figure out how to ask you two if you'd mind me eating your shares, too."

"You sure were concentrating on it." Zach's smile was kind instead of knowing. "All you had to do was ask."

But Rita shook her head. "Too much food. That is not good—"

Pilar interrupted her with a wave of her hand. "Just kidding, *Mami*."

Her mother responded with a curt nod. Though she'd been speaking English since she and Salvador had moved from the U.S. Commonwealth of Puerto Rico right after they were married, Rita still preferred the language of her birth and hadn't mastered all of the intricacies of humor in her second language. She was often embarrassed when she didn't understand jokes.

Pilar floundered for a way to ease the awkward moment and decided to offer the blessing, but just as she opened her mouth to speak, a warm hand curled around hers. Her breath caught in her throat and her heart beat so loudly in her ears that everyone in the room—and maybe even in the apartment across the hall—must have heard.

Confusion rolled through her thoughts. Why had he chosen this moment to finally hold her hand? She didn't even have to ask herself if she liked it. Her skin positively thrummed at the point of contact, and already she mourned the moment he would release her fingers.

But Zach seemed oblivious to the storm crashing through her thoughts. He only closed his eyes and lowered his head. To pray. Too late, Pilar noticed that Zach held her mother's fine-fingered hand with his other one. Her face had to be so red that she was as thankful for the closed-eyed act of praying as much as the food.

"Lord, thank You for Your promise to always be with us," Zach began. "Thank You for blessings we acknowledge and the many we take for granted. Please bless this food and provide healing in this home. Amen."

"Amen," Rita repeated as the three of them released hands.

Rita smiled at Zach for so long that Pilar became embarrassed all over again. Zach nodded before turning his attention back to the food. He doled out small servings from a few containers and passed them around.

While he took his first bite with his left hand, he slipped his other one, the one with which he'd touched Pilar, under the table to wipe on his pants leg. The hand that had held her sweaty palm. So now he either had problems with his sweat glands or he recognized how nervous she was.

"You're left-handed," Pilar blurted before she could stop herself. She couldn't have made it more obvious that she'd been watching him. She wondered if she would die of embarrassment before they even ate their fortune cookies.

"Aren't all creative-thinking people?"

"No," Pilar and Rita chorused and then laughed. At least something had lightened the mood.

"Probably some are," Pilar conceded.

"Thank you." He returned to his food, swishing a piece of deep-fried pork in sweet-and-sour sauce.

"Speaking of creative thinking, were there any new developments in the case today?"

He shook his head. "No breaks." He stared down at his plate for several seconds before looking back at her, his frustrated frown replaced with a grin. "I did drop by to see Gabriel today at lunch. He's being a real trooper about all this."

Zach must have noticed her questioning expression because he rushed on. "He's already looking bigger. Some of those crinkled baby folds are smoothing out, and those eyes— He's really sharp. I can tell."

"Police talk to a *bebé, sí?*"

Pilar and Zach both turned back to Rita, who looked as confused as Pilar felt. Of course, her mother didn't understand why a detective would spend valuable investigation time talking to a newborn.

He turned to Rita and shook his head, losing his battle not to smile at the question. "Oh, no. It was just a visit on my lunch hour."

But his expression was serious when he turned back

to Pilar. "I didn't want him to get too lonely since he didn't have his regular lunch visitor."

Why he'd visited Gabriel suddenly made sense. He'd done it for her. Well, maybe not completely for her. He might have visited the Frasers' in part as a reminder of the young life affected by his investigation's outcome. He might even have gone out of guilt. But at least part of the reason he'd taken time out of his day was to stand in for Pilar with the baby she adored. Though he'd probably only intended it as a polite gesture, his action wrapped itself around her heart.

"I told Reverend Fraser and Naomi you were going to be busy for a few days."

Once again he was taking care of her, making the situation easier for her, even if he couldn't make it all go away. An image filtered into her thoughts then of that first day at Tiny Blessings where he'd wrapped his jacket around her shoulders and she'd given it back to him. Next, she felt the lightness of being carried in his arms, felt his kindness delivered in noodle soup and peanut butter. She hadn't fought his care so hard that time.

This was so out of character for her. Giving, now she understood that. She was used to reaching out to friends and strangers alike and praying for God to use her to help those in need. But receiving? That was a whole different story.

She was an independent woman. She didn't need anyone to take care of her. And yet it didn't seem so unsuitable accepting when the hands reaching out to her were Zach's. Why was it that accepting his help, even resting in his capable arms when the occasion called for it, made her feel safe and free at the same time?

"Thanks." She said it for so many reasons, his sweet gesture only one of them.

He nodded but didn't look away, as she'd expected. She knew she should, but Pilar couldn't pull away her gaze, either. Her breath caught. Time stopped.

The sound of chair legs scraping over linoleum, though, dropped reality back into the center of the Formica tabletop. Pilar turned toward the sound of her mother pushing away from the table. Zach pushed back and stood, as well, his good manners ingrained.

Pilar realized she'd been wrong. She hadn't had all the embarrassment a person could handle in one day. Her cheeks didn't even bother to burn this time. Overuse had worn out their steam.

She shot a glance at Zach, who appeared as wide-eyed as she must have looked.

Rita didn't glance at either of them but started clearing away the dishes and containers.

"*Mami,* I'll get those."

Pilar started to stand, but her mother waved her hand to stop her. "Nonsense. It takes little time."

"Here, let me help." Zach carried glasses to the sink, but Rita only took them out of his hands and shooed him from the kitchenette, insisting there wasn't enough room there for two.

With the same efficiency that had always amazed Pilar while she was growing up, her mother was finished and was wiping her hands on a towel only minutes later. She gathered her Bible-study materials from the counter and headed to the slider.

"I must finish my lesson before it gets dark. I need quiet. You stay here." With that she stepped out the door and closed it behind her.

"Do you think we've been dismissed?"

When Pilar turned back to Zach, he raised an eyebrow.

She shook her head, her insides shaky. "I'm not sure what that was about."

She had an idea, but she wasn't positive, and her guess wasn't making any sense at all. Her mother had always made a point of *not* playing matchmaker. Why would she change that now?

"I could go, I guess."

"Who would I talk to then?" It was easier to ask that question than to admit she didn't want him to leave, so she went with it. "My mother said she needed quiet. I shouldn't interrupt her."

"No, shouldn't do that."

She was relieved the moment he settled back in the side chair and kicked off his shoes, signs that he was staying. Sure, it felt a little silly with her mother right outside the door as an official chaperone, but inside it was just the two of them. So for the second day in a row, Zach and Pilar discussed everything and nothing, laughing, talking and laughing some more, until the sun disappeared from Chestnut Grove.

A telephone ring Friday afternoon interrupted the silence that had reminded Pilar of the hollow sound inside an empty church sanctuary. Only she liked the church when it was empty because it always felt like having a private audience in God's presence. Her apartment, though, felt empty and nothing more.

"Hello," she called into the receiver, hoping and yet trying not to hope over the caller's identity.

"Well, you sound okay."

Pilar's breath hitched at the sound of Zach's voice, but a smile lifted her lips and her heart. She could hear the laughter in his voice and could easily picture him smiling, too. She'd seen it enough the last three days to perfect the memory in her mind.

"I sound okay because I am okay." She sat down in a dining chair with barely more than a pinch in her belly.

"Then why weren't you at the office today?"

She shrugged though he couldn't see her. "Since I'd already taken off until Monday, I decided to wait."

"Did you see Gabriel today?"

"Same reason."

"Sounds sensible."

"That's me, Miss Sensible."

He didn't even debate her on it but instead asked, "Is your mom still there with you?"

"No, she went home this morning. She figured *Papi* had suffered from bachelorhood long enough."

"Does the apartment feel empty now?"

*You have no idea,* she wanted to say. But she only answered, "A little." Until this week, her apartment had felt like her own private retreat. She'd liked being alone in it. But something had changed. Everything had changed.

She wouldn't lie to herself by suggesting her loneliness had only to do with her mother's leaving. It was about an end to these last three horrible yet wonderful days that had taken place in a vacuum. It was about Zach and the unfortunate fact that she'd come to care for him too much.

Even with the discomfort, she wouldn't trade these last few days, as they'd been three of her best. She loved spending time with Zach, sharing stories, discussing the case and playing board games while *Mami* always found excuses to stay outside on the balcony. Zach, though, had made a point not to leave Rita out, even bringing the fixings and making huge ice-cream sundaes for all of them.

She'd sensed a couple of times that Zach was holding something back, especially about his parents, who he had admitted he hadn't spoken to in a long time. But who was she to question his reluctance to talk about it? He'd respected her privacy until she was ready to share her troubles with him. She had every intention of showing that same kind of patience and being the same kind of friend he'd been to her.

Would she ever get the chance to be that friend, though? Would she ever have the opportunity to spend time with him again now that *Mami* had returned to her real life and Pilar had no excuse but to return to hers? Her heart ached with the loss to come.

"But there isn't any reason you can't get out of that empty place," Zach was saying when his words finally filtered back into her thoughts.

"Uh, sorry. What did you say?"

"That you don't have to stay in that apartment now. That you can get out, and you don't have to wait until church on Sunday."

Pilar's pulse raced. He was only making conversation, she reminded herself. He was only suggesting that she get out, not that she should go anywhere with him.

"I guess I could. Maybe I'll drop by and see Gabriel tomorrow." She didn't want him to feel guilty over leaving her alone this weekend. She could take his unknowing rejection the way she'd experienced it before, but she still didn't want his pity.

Zach cleared his throat, clearly as uncomfortable as she was. "I was talking about tonight."

"What do you mean?" Could her heart beat any faster, and could her throat feel any tighter?

He cleared his throat again, but when he spoke, his words were crystal clear. "Since you feel well enough to go out now, I would like you to go out with me…on a date."

# *Chapter Eleven*

Zach turned his face into the wind whipped up by Richmond's Kanawha Canal and wondered how a person could be that excited and that terrified at the same time. His stomach rolled, but it probably wasn't from the boat's steady journey along the canal that linked the Kanawha River with the James River, which in turn flowed into the Ohio.

"Hey, are you okay? You look a little green." Pilar's eyebrows knit together in concern.

"Just getting my sea legs." Neither mentioned that he wasn't even standing, but was seated at the table in the canvas-topped canal boat. He hoped the queasiness was only a little seasickness, but he had to wonder if he'd feel just as unstable on dry land. He was so out of his element, there hadn't been a phrase invented yet to quantify it.

Pilar sighed. "You were right. This is beautiful." Taking a bite of her chicken, she wiped her mouth on her napkin and sighed again.

She turned her profile to him, staring out at the well-maintained landscaping and lovingly restored historic buildings along the canal system. A few dark tresses that had escaped the plait down Pilar's back fluttered against her cheek. Something was beautiful, all right, but it was the woman who sat right there in the boat. Peace settled over him as he sat with her, giving him the unfamiliar sense that all was right in the world.

"It was a great idea coming here. How did you ever think of it?"

A whole night of poring over Richmond travel brochures, but he didn't want to admit that. Since he figured he had a ridiculous grin on his face, he was grateful she was still watching the water instead of him. He'd wanted to plan something special for her, and dinner out just hadn't seemed special enough.

A big gesture was necessary to top the food he'd plied her with in her recovery, and a private charter dinner boat from Richmond's Turning Basin was nothing if not creative. Unfortunately, the charter costs depleted his salary, so he'd had to forego the caterers the charter service had suggested in favor of a picnic basket and his regular standby of fried chicken from the Starlight. It was cold now, but Pilar didn't seem to mind. He couldn't help grinning and being inordinately pleased that she'd liked his surprise.

"You're telling me your other first dates haven't been

on the water like this one?" Out of his peripheral vision, he watched her shake her head.

"You told me this was supposed to be a historically narrated tour."

"That was optional on the private charters. But if you need a history lesson, I can tell you the Richmond riverfront is one and a quarter miles long, beginning at the Tredegar Iron Works site."

A grin on her face, Pilar waved her hand to stop him.

"Are you sure you don't want to know how George Washington appeared before the Virginia General Assembly in 1784 to support legislation for a canal system to bypass the falls?"

Pilar quirked her head. "How do you know all that?"

"It says it right here on the brochure." He produced the page he'd printed from the Internet site to impress her.

"I'll be sure to store these facts for later."

"You do that. You never know when you'll be called upon for Richmond Canal trivia."

Zach took a forkful of coleslaw, and Pilar quieted as well while they ate. The world around them was far from silent though, with sounds of birds flying overhead and tourists strolling along the River Walk melding with the swish of rushing waters to create a soothing hum.

"You know, it's funny," Pilar said as she set her napkin aside. "This doesn't feel like a first date."

She was right; the night felt nothing like a first date. He tried not to let that reality scare him. It felt as if they'd spent years, rather than hours, getting to know each other, and he sensed that even after a quarter century or more, he would still love just listening to her stories. What was he to do with that knowledge?

He couldn't help it, though. He craved information about her. What kind of books did she read? Other than her study Bible and concordance on the table, he wasn't sure. What made her smile when she didn't know anyone was watching? If his guess was right, he already knew the answer to that one. Him.

He'd caught those furtive glances enough to guess, even if he hadn't suspected from the first time he'd held her hand to pray. His own hand had tingled for five minutes, as though it had been asleep when he'd touched her satiny skin.

Yes, he knew she had feelings for him, but he was far less sure he was strong enough to handle the responsibility that her care placed on him. She was so trusting and so sweetly naive in the way she believed people would do the right thing even when they had more tempting alternatives. He'd been on the police force long enough to know better. He tried not to envy her the easy way she trusted in others, though he wondered if it would have been easier for him if his scars weren't so deep.

Why out of every man in the world had Pilar chosen him when another man might have been able to fully care for her in a way he couldn't? Or could he? He wasn't sure, but he did know he was jealous of that hypothetical "other man" who might try.

Zach glanced across the table again, catching her studying him. Her awed expression surprised him. He didn't deserve her gratitude for coming by a few times when his intentions had been so selfish. Spending time with her had made him happier than he'd been in a long time, and he'd been helpless but to return again and again.

Though Gabriel had grown on him and he'd gotten a kick out of visiting the little guy, he'd at first only gone because he'd wanted to see Pilar smile when he told her about it. Selfish again.

Guilt riddled the peace he'd enjoyed while sitting close enough to catch the honeyed scent of her hair. Though she'd shared her secret and had opened her thoughts and feelings to him, he'd kept his own stories buried inside. He knew Pilar, but he hadn't allowed her to know him at all.

"You didn't tell me, did you get by to see Gabriel today?"

Zach felt his Adam's apple shift as he swallowed. She couldn't possibly have known what he'd been thinking about. She'd asked after Gabriel each day when he'd come by, obviously missing the baby. But God knew what was on his mind, and Zach could feel Him suggesting that the time to share his story had arrived.

"I dropped by at lunch. Naomi let me give him a bottle."

Pilar smiled. "Did you get it all over you?"

He shook his head. It would have been so easy to keep talking about the baby, without ever revealing what lay heavily on his heart. But Zach couldn't hold it inside any longer. The walls he'd built around his feelings were strained and worn, and he could think of nothing he wanted more than to finally let them fall.

"There's something I want to tell you about Gabriel's case." His throat burned with the admission, but it was finally out there between them where he couldn't take it back. He didn't even want to.

Her eyes widened and her arms crossed as if to protect herself from the cold, though she already wore a jacket. "What is it? Did you find his mother?"

He shook his head with regret. "No. Not yet. This is something else."

Instead of asking a question he could have used to delay telling her, she simply stared at him and waited.

"Remember when you asked me if I take all cases this personally?"

"I remember."

"Well, I don't. I'm usually great at separating myself from them. Compartmentalizing."

She nodded. "Of course. It's part of your job."

It was part of hers, too, but he doubted Pilar had ever compartmentalized anything about one of the babies or children she'd placed. She probably took every story home with her. It was just who she was.

Again, he could have escaped telling her and could have talked about police work instead. This was too important though. He wanted her to know, needed to finally share with someone he knew would care.

"I can't separate myself this time. I should never have accepted this case. I'm taking it personally because that's what it is—personal."

Pilar could only stare at him, her throat tight. What was he trying to say? That he knew Gabriel's mother? That he could have answered the questions in the investigation all along?

Theories whirled through her mind, each crazier than the last. Was he covering for someone to prevent a scandal? Had he been threatened if he revealed the truth? Or was it even *more* personal than that?

He must have recognized the spinning wheels in her thoughts because the side of his mouth lifted. "No, the baby isn't mine. I don't even know the mother."

"Then what is it about this baby?"

He shrugged and sat quietly for long enough that she figured he wouldn't answer.

"It isn't about *this* baby."

"I don't understand."

Zach stared past her at the riverbank for several seconds before turning back to her. "There's no way you could understand unless you knew Jasmine, my sister."

Realization settled over her and her throat constricted. "Did your sister have a baby?"

"Just like…this time." His voice sounded strained.

"You mean she abandoned her baby?"

"My niece died." He swallowed a few times and turned his head away. "So did Jasmine."

Pilar drew in a sudden breath and stiffened. Anguish

on behalf of Zach, his sister and the child that had been lost washed over her.

"Oh, Zach, I'm so sorry." Before she could stop herself, she clasped her hand over his forearm.

Instead of pushing her away as she'd worried he would, he rested his other hand on top of hers.

He cleared his throat and tried again. "She was just sixteen—two years younger than I was. At first Jasmine hid her pregnancy. Our parents were furious when they found out."

"Oh, how awful for all of you," she said, squeezing his arm when what she wanted to do was draw him into the circle of her arms and let him fully experience the grief he'd probably buried for years.

He continued as if he hadn't heard her, his eyes dry despite the tragedy he told. "There was this huge fight, and Jasmine ran away from home. I didn't do anything…to stop her."

Zach tilted his head back in that strange, tight way men have of fighting tears. The boat captain and single crew member pretended not to notice the tough, masculine man whose composure had disintegrated.

Her heart broke for the wounded teenager he must have been and for the scarred man he'd become. She held his hand between both of hers, giving what comfort she could.

"You know it wasn't your fault, don't you? You were just a kid yourself."

But he didn't answer. Maybe he didn't realize he

was a victim just as much as the rest of his family. That the circumstances were beyond his control. Or if he did accept it rationally, he didn't believe it in his heart, where it counted.

He didn't look at her, but kept talking. Maybe now that he'd started, he had to say it all.

"The baby was premature," he continued. "Jasmine tried to do the right thing. She left her baby on the hospital steps, but March was still cold that year, and Angela died of exposure."

"Angela?"

"My parents named her so there would be a name on the birth certificate. It means 'angel.'" He finally met her gaze, his eyes again dry. "They're buried right next to each other."

Surely, Zach didn't believe his niece and his sister, if she was a believer, were in those plots of dirt where their bodies had been placed. Pilar knew him well enough now to be certain of that. But his thoughts seemed somewhere other than eternity at that moment, and she didn't know how to help him.

"How did Jasmine die?"

"The police found her on a park bench, suffering from blood loss and exposure. They rushed her to the hospital, but it was already too late."

"I'm so sorry. What a horrible tragedy for your family. I can't imagine the loss your parents must feel."

"Their loss?" His voice boomed, so Zach repeated those words again more quietly. "Their loss. They caused that loss. Two people had to die because they couldn't be embarrassed in front of their church friends."

"That's probably a mistake they've regretted every day of their lives."

He shook his head. "Some things you just can't take back, and there aren't any do-overs."

She wanted to tell him he was wrong because no sin was too big for God to forgive. But Zach was right that some things could never be undone. Gabriel's mother, for instance, could spend the next eighteen years trying to make up for her mistake, but she could never erase the fact that she'd left her son on a porch out in the cold.

It was the same way for Zach's parents. Though God had forgiven them for their part in the tragedy, they'd never be able to take back the hateful things they'd said to their daughter.

"That's an awful thing to have to live with," she said when Zach seemed to expect a response.

"They deserve a lot of sleepless nights."

They'd probably had more than their share of those, but Pilar didn't see any point in telling Zach that. They'd probably never forgiven themselves, and even if they'd somehow made peace with their mistakes, their son would never let them forget. He blamed his parents almost as much as he blamed himself. Their pride had cost them not one, but both of their children. She couldn't even imagine that kind of loss.

"Where are your parents now?"

"Still in Philadelphia. But that's not far enough as far as I'm concerned."

Zach turned his head away then, his jaw flexed from gritted teeth, the vein in his temple visible. She watched him, her heart aching for his pain and for the anger that hurt him just as much.

How could she have been so selfish? She'd been so focused on her own fears about not having a child and how those fears coincided with Gabriel's arrival that she hadn't even recognized that others involved might have had scars of their own. Even Gabriel's mother probably had a sad story to tell. Zach's story shamed her most of all. Her personal pain felt small compared to all he'd lost.

"Isn't it exhausting?" she asked him when she could no longer keep her thoughts to herself.

"What do you mean?" He did look tired when he turned back to her. Opening to her had cost him. That much was clear. She wondered if the price tag had been too high. Would he pull away from her just when he'd finally allowed her a peek inside his troubled heart?

"Keeping all that anger inside has to be tiring."

His posture tightened, and Pilar braced herself for that anger to be projected toward her in words that would hurt. But after several long seconds, Zach curled his shoulders forward again. He looked so defeated that she felt helpless with the need to make it better for him.

"As I said, some things can't be taken back," he said finally.

"But forgiveness can be given as a free gift the way God gives it. Maybe you'll never be able to forget what your parents did, but you can forgive them."

He glanced at her from underneath his eyelashes, his expression softening. "I've tried that. It didn't go well."

"Maybe that's something you should turn over to God."

His lips pulled up, and he met her gaze. "That's pretty good advice. Maybe you should try it. You know, that whole 'physician heal thyself' thing."

Guilt threatening to seep into her thoughts, Pilar opened her mouth to disagree with him. Their problems were different. Zach, though, only shook his head to stop her.

"You know as well as I do that the only way the situation is ever going to be okay is if you let God handle it." He paused, and his voice was gentle when he spoke again. "Babies or no babies, He'll make it okay."

Her eyes burned, but she couldn't let herself cry again, not when Zach was right. "I know it's what I need to do, but I think I've been selfish with my worries just as I was selfish with my secret."

"It's a whole lot easier to give that advice than to take it, isn't it?"

Pilar couldn't help chuckling. "We're quite a pair, aren't we?"

"Yes, we are."

Her laughter caught in her throat as she met his gaze again. He didn't look away. She couldn't have if she'd tried. She sensed that he wasn't talking about the pair of stumbling Christians who rode along the canal's clear path while their personal lives floated adrift. Did he really see them like that: as a couple? Could she even dare to believe he would return her feelings?

Her hands sweaty again, Pilar reached for her paper napkin and wiped them. What was she supposed to do now? Should she say something funny to lighten the moment? Already, she wondered why the night sky settling around them didn't glimmer with sparks from the electricity on the boat's deck.

"Would you mind if I came over and sat by you?" Zach's gaze never left her as he asked the question. "I'd like to see the sights from the same vantage point."

She nodded, not trusting herself to speak.

Zach moved his chair next to hers, not too close, but close enough that she found it difficult to breathe. On what little oxygen she drew into her lungs, his masculine scent tantalized her nostrils. Even if their sweet story ended there, she imagined she would carry his scent in her memory as part of the most wonderful night of her life.

But he reached for her hand, and the memory blossomed with the potential for more. His fingers curled around hers in a perfect, loving fit, so different from the other time they'd joined hands in prayer. This time hearts were involved, at least hers was, and she wanted to believe his was, as well. So acutely aware of his history, she was surprised he had the courage to reach out to anyone. She felt honored and blessed that he'd chosen her.

She longed to speak, to ask him to explain what his touch meant. Was he reaching out for comfort from her, or had his feelings for her become tender? She couldn't ask, though, couldn't risk shattering the moment that formed liked a goblet of blown glass, still warm and fragile.

Their hands folded together, Zach traced his thumb along the side of hers in a trancelike rhythm until the scenery around them, the night sky above the buildings and the chilly waters beneath the boat seemed to disappear, leaving only the two of them together.

"Pilar." His voice sounded strange.

"Yes?"

"Would you mind if I kissed you?"

The sound that erupted in her throat shamed her as it sounded too much like laughter. Mind? How could she mind something when she'd dreamed of it hundreds of times without ever once expecting it to happen? When he turned his head to study her, she was grateful for the retreating daylight and the opportunity to hide her embarrassment behind the night sky.

"I'd like that," she somehow managed.

Releasing her hand, Zach traced that same thumb under her jaw and then tilted her chin upward. She let her eyes flutter closed but still she sensed his nearness growing by tiny increments until his lips covered hers.

So sweet, so gentle, his kiss was unassuming. Not rushed but lingering like a message he'd held inside for a long time and wanted to tell it well. She'd imagined what kissing Zach would be like so many times, but her fantasy didn't even come close to the real thing.

It was only a kiss, she reminded herself, but it felt like something more. A promise. Of what, she wasn't positive, though her heart hoped.

"I've wanted to do that for a long time." He breathed the words against her cheek.

Her breath caught in her throat as he brushed his lips over hers twice more. Too soon, the kiss was over, but at the same time it was too late for Pilar not to have been positive about what she'd been suspecting all along. She was in love with Zach—not the image she'd had of him until a week ago but the real flesh-and-blood man she'd come to know.

She didn't even want that other man anymore, so untouchable in his perfection. This Zach had flaws every bit as real as her own, and they only made him more precious to her.

Pilar's heart squeezed as the captain announced their approach to the docking site and the end to their romantic canal cruise. If only the waters would stop rushing forward, pushing them to their destination. She wasn't asking for much. She only wanted this time to last a little longer.

Tomorrow things could be different. Maybe Zach would realize that all of it—the date, his confiding in her, even the kiss—had been a mistake. She didn't know what the future would hold. She only knew she didn't want this night to end.

## Chapter Twelve

Zach stared after the last pair of taillights that disappeared Sunday night from Chestnut Grove Community Church's parking lot and then turned back to Pilar. Theirs were the only two cars that remained in the fluorescent-lit lot after the evening service.

"Did you see the way Reverend Fraser was looking at us?" Pilar covered her face with her hands but spread her fingers enough to still peek out at him.

Zach grinned. If she was embarrassed by the minister's mild curiosity, then she hadn't been paying close attention to the rest of the people in the sanctuary. He and Pilar were probably the talk of the congregation by now, having sat together during two consecutive services.

He considered mentioning the knowing glance Naomi Fraser had tossed his way following the evening benediction, but he decided against it. Pilar seemed embarrassed enough for one day.

"He was just trying to get us to go home."

"And gave up." Pilar glanced at the empty space where the minister's car had last been.

"He probably figured we could use a few minutes alone. I know I did." With a sly grin, he reached for her hand and pulled her until she leaned on his car next to him.

At least she hadn't said she was sick of him. He couldn't blame her, as much time as they'd spent together the last few days. Between dates on Friday and Saturday nights and two church services Sunday, they'd managed to fit in a joint visit with Gabriel Saturday afternoon.

Still, although he'd seen more of Pilar than of any human being in that forty-eight-hour period, he was only searching for other ways to spend more time with her. She'd become a habit, but he didn't even want to break it.

Pilar glanced down at their laced fingers and then looked up at him and smiled.

"So how did your brunch go?"

She shrugged. "I told them."

"And?"

"They're my friends. They forgave me. It's in the friendship manual, I'm pretty sure."

"Fortunately for you, they'd read the manual." He chuckled and then became serious. "Did your friends tell you everything would be all right?"

She nodded. "Meg even said we should all pray for God's comfort and healing. You never would have heard that from her until a few months ago."

"You've got some good friends."

"I do." She paused and looked at him from under her lashes. "Including you."

He raised an eyebrow but wasn't sure whether she could see it. "Is that what we are? Friends?"

"It's a start," she answered in a soft voice.

"Yes, it is." Only Zach wanted to be so much more to Pilar. He wanted to be the person she couldn't wait to tell when wonderful things happened to her and the one whose arms she turned to when she was hurting. He wanted to be the man she trusted with her heart.

His own emotions had been on a roller coaster from the moment he'd first faced Pilar and the foundling, but he didn't want to lift the safety bar and exit the ride. When his feelings for her, that began with curiosity, had expanded to concern and then commitment, he wasn't sure. But they had changed whether he was ready for it or not.

Without any use of excessive force, Pilar had crashed through the wall he'd built around his heart ever since Jasmine had died. He'd found, much to his surprise, that his ability to love hadn't died along with her.

*I love you.* The words burned on his lips to be spoken, so why couldn't he say them aloud? Whether he spoke them or not, he couldn't deny the feelings in his heart. But as much as he wanted to be, was he ready to put his trust in someone else?

Alone, he'd felt invincible, as if he'd had something stronger than even a Kevlar vest to protect his heart. He didn't want to be safe anymore. He wanted to really know Pilar and, for the first time, to let someone else really know him. More than anything, he wanted to finally put his trust and his hope in the woman he loved.

Still, the words wouldn't come, so he expressed his feelings without them. Drawing Pilar into his arms, he kissed her gently, all the feelings of his heart laid bare for her. She slid her hands over his shoulders to lace behind his neck in a wonderful gift of trust.

Zach lifted his head away but still held her close so that her cheek rested against his chest. If only the beating of his heart could convey that he carried her with him inside.

"This is nice," she murmured.

"Yeah." He lightly stroked her hair with his fingertips.

Pilar lifted her head to face him again. "It's back to reality again tomorrow, isn't it?"

Reality. Clearly, she'd been talking about her own difficult return to work. Still, he couldn't help but turn that question on himself. What had he done this weekend to put himself any closer to finding Gabriel's mother? Which lead had he pursued? What tip had he followed up on? Since the answer was unequivocally *none,* he didn't even try to make excuses for himself.

All weekend he'd selfishly spent nearly every minute outside work with Pilar when he could have been putting in extra hours on the investigation. They were no closer to locating Gabriel's mother than that first day at the adoption agency, and he had no one to blame but himself.

"Back to reality, all right. I'm going to be pretty busy—"

Pilar took an abrupt step back from him, stopping him midsentence. "Oh...don't worry about it."

For a few seconds, he only stared at her blankly. When what she really meant dawned on him, he was mystified by it. After all the hours they'd spent together, could she still believe she was just a charity case to him?

Didn't she realize he couldn't get enough of seeing her smile, feeling her laughter wash over him or listening to her voice? She could only see that he'd played nursemaid to her, but his heart had begun to heal with the touch of her gentle hand.

"Worry about the case?" He tried not to smile at having purposely misunderstood her. "I'll keep worrying about it until I find the answers I need."

She was already shaking her head when he reached out to her and tucked a few stray strands of her hair behind her ear.

"I've been...preoccupied this weekend, so I'll have to refocus my efforts on the case. I won't be able to call you—" he paused as he watched her nod again, too easily giving up on him "—at least until tomorrow night."

He took her surprised expression as his cue to draw her into his arms once more. Pilar was right. They were quite a pair. He was afraid of trusting someone with his heart, and she questioned whether she was worthy of it. He only hoped that God, in His infinite wisdom, would help them find a way to be strong together.

The Tiny Blessings office hadn't changed much in a week without her, but that Monday morning as Pilar glanced about it, she realized that *she* was different. She even hazarded a glance at the Wall of Blessings, but instead of the pain she'd expected, peace filled her heart. She grinned back at the rows of smiling faces. *Thank You, Father.*

She owed it to Zach that she was beginning to turn over her fears to God. Now she could see that God had been with her all through the crisis, even sending Zach to her just when she needed a friend. The story ran full circle when her friend helped her to trust God again.

She must have been smiling because when Anne passed her, she cocked her head and raised an eyebrow.

"Glad to have you back, sweetie. Are you feeling okay?"

Pilar grinned. "I'm fine. Really."

The ringing phone interrupted their conversation, and Anne crossed the room to answer it. She pointed to the phone before she lifted the handset. "We're getting positive calls again ever since Jared's newspaper series started running Friday."

As Anne spoke into the phone, Pilar returned to the files on her desk. Two new couples had applied for adoption while she'd been off work. One was even interested in a special-needs child. She couldn't wait to set up their interviews and home visits.

"Detective Fletcher's on line two for you."

Her friend wore a silly grin when Pilar looked up, one that probably resembled hers. Could her suspicion be right? Could Zach be the man God had planned for her all along?

"Hello, Zach." Her breath caught in her throat as she waited to hear his voice. So deeply embedded in her memory now, she guessed that even in a crowded and darkened room, she could still find him as soon as he spoke.

"Hey, Pilar."

She cleared her throat and glanced around to see if Kelly was looking out from her office. She didn't have to look to know that Anne was watching. "I, um, thought I wouldn't hear from you until tonight."

"Sorry. This is business."

She straightened in her seat, sensing that whatever he was about to tell her wasn't good. "Okay."

"I just wanted to tell you that there's been a break in the case."

Zach put the phone down again Monday afternoon, annoyed by the frustration that he couldn't seem to set aside. The Tarkington Academy flyer lay in the center of his desk, taunting him. The fancy gold lettering embossed on it was new to him, but the paper it was printed on, he would have recognized that anywhere.

He should have been relieved that there was finally a break in the case. But the fact that rookie cop Steve Merritt had been the one to make the connection just didn't set right with him. He felt guilty knowing Steve had been putting in the extra time over the weekend while Zach had been focused on his love life.

Steve popped by his desk then as he'd been doing all day, that annoying grin of achievement never leaving his face. "Any more developments, Detective?"

"Well, it's confirmed that the flyer was produced by Guffy's Printing on Main. We also have a list of students who served on the open house committee and helped to design the flyer."

"That's pretty good progress for one day."

"Couldn't have done it without you, buddy."

The junior officer's eyes widened at the comment, and he nodded. No doubt he could relate to how hard that compliment had been to give, and he appreciated the effort. Steve lifted the flyer off the desk and studied it as if he might find something new on it.

"And to think that we might never have made the connection if I hadn't gone to my sister's for dinner Saturday."

"What do you mean?" At least the junior officer wasn't really working off-duty like he'd suspected.

"Becky's trying to squeeze her ex-husband out of more support money by sending my niece to the most exclusive private high school in Chestnut Grove."

"Great. Now we benefit from the after-ripples of a nasty divorce."

"We take it where we can get it."

Zach shrugged. The rookie was right. It might turn out to be just another dead end like every other lead, but they would take it and be grateful if it finally led to their suspect.

"What's next?" Steve seemed to be getting a kick out of his opportunity to do more than take initial reports.

"I'm waiting for word back from Tarkington Academy. I'll be going in this afternoon to interview all seven students on the list."

"Even the boys?" Steve raised an eyebrow. "Unlikely moms, I would guess."

"They might be witnesses, or one of them might be the long-lost dad."

Zach's desk phone rang then, so he held up an index finger to let Steve know he'd get back to him momentarily. As he jotted down notes from the school's headmaster, he caught movement in his peripheral vision. Pilar came through the door and paused at the front desk. He tried to focus on his telephone conversation, but he couldn't keep his eyes off her.

Why was she here? He'd shared with her that there had been a break in the case because he'd figured she would want to know, but the last thing he'd expected was for her to show up at the station. He couldn't blame her, though. She was tied to the case on so many levels.

"Could you spell that last name again, Headmaster Douglas?"

He tried to pay attention this time so he didn't have to ask the oh-so-formal Elliot Douglas III to repeat it a third time. The educator was already annoyed enough that police would be interrupting his students for interviews that probably didn't involve them.

"Okay, H-a-r-c-o-u-r-t," he spelled back to Douglas. "Thank you so much. I'll meet you in your office at one."

When he glanced at the front desk, Pilar was no longer standing there. Across the room, though, he found her sitting in the visitor's chair next to Steve's desk and talking to him. He surprised himself, as he probably had them, by crossing to the other desk in about eight annoyed strides.

Steve popped up like an army private snapping to attention, and Pilar just stared.

*Pull yourself together, Fletcher.* He forced a smile and patted Steve's shoulder. Already, Zach didn't like himself much that day for resenting the other officer's discovery, but now he'd reacted like a jealous jerk. If his day was starting out this bad, he could only imagine how long he'd be on his knees praying for forgiveness that night.

"Hi, Pilar. Did Officer Merritt tell you how he found the brochure?"

She smiled and nodded at Steve. "Good thing for dinner at your sister's." Then she turned back to Zach, her expression unreadable.

Because she didn't say anything, he finally asked, "Were you here to see me?"

At her nervous glance toward the other officer, Zach put his hand under her elbow to guide her to his desk. "What is it? Did you find something else at the office?"

She shook her head. "I had to come. I wasn't helpful before, so I want to do anything I can now."

He smiled, remembering that she initially hadn't wanted him to find Gabriel's mother.

"Not much you can do really. I'll be interviewing the open house committee members this afternoon. Everyone except a girl who's on a European vacation with her parents." He glanced down at the list and read the name. "Ashley Harcourt."

He looked up to see Pilar's eyes widen at the same time that the name was starting ringing a bell in his mind.

"Why does that name sound so—wait. Is she any relation to Barnaby Harcourt?"

"His granddaughter. Neal and Helene's daughter."

It wasn't such an amazing coincidence that a Harcourt would attend Tarkington Academy. They were, after all, among the wealthiest families in Chestnut Grove. But in his experience, odd coincidences in investigations often didn't turn out to be only that.

"Do you know when the Harcourts are supposed to get back from their trip?"

Pilar shook her head. "I don't know them personally, but my friend Rachel does. They're friends with her parents. Let me give her a call." She went to the phone Zach indicated on a nearby desk and started dialing.

While he waited, Zach scanned the list of names. Obviously, he didn't travel in the same circles as the well-heeled because he didn't recognize any other names.

He glanced up to see Pilar hang up the phone, but her strange expression stopped him.

"What is it?"

She came back over and dropped into the chair next to his desk. "Rachel said Neal and Helene were supposed to be gone four weeks."

He lifted his notebook and pen. "Starting when?"

When she didn't say anything, he glanced at her.

"That's just it. Only the two of them went on the trip. Helene joked about it being a romantic getaway, but Rachel's mom had been worried it was a last-ditch effort to save their troubled marriage."

That same unsettled feeling he always developed when stories and facts weren't adding up wrapped itself around him, making him straighten. He knew Pilar had picked up on the change in him because she, too, sat a little higher in her chair.

"If they went alone, where's the rest of the family?" he asked as calmly as possible.

"Samantha's working as a catalogue model in D.C., but Ashley? She's supposed to be at home and attending school."

"School's the one place we know she hasn't been. We'd better find out if she's been at the other one."

"Do you think she's a runaway?"

Zach tilted his head and considered. "Could be."

Ashley wouldn't have been the first teen from a wealthy but dysfunctional family to do that. It also wouldn't have necessarily followed that just because she might have run she was also the person targeted in this investigation, but Zach sensed she was. He didn't need more coincidences to convince him since his churning gut and his critical thinking agreed this time.

He grabbed his keys and his notebook but paused by the door. "The Harcourt mansion, right?"

Pilar nodded.

"Zach, I think you'd better take this call," the receptionist announced from the front desk.

On the other end of the line, a small Richmond clinic—one where needs were high, resources were low and returning detectives' telephone calls apparently wasn't a priority—had finally checked in.

"Detective, you were looking for births from the last few weeks," said a harried doctor, who'd probably attended to dozens of deliveries in that time. "Our clinic had a walker on September first. Her name and address didn't check out."

"Can you describe her?" Zach grabbed his notebook even though he was pretty sure a description wouldn't be necessary.

"Age sixteen or seventeen. Caucasian. Blond hair in braids."

"And the infant."

"Live birth on eight-thirty-one. Healthy male. She disappeared with the infant the next morning after his circumcision."

Zach indicated with a wave for Officer Merritt to take over the call and make up the report for him. On his way past the front desk, he slammed his fist on the counter.

"A day late and a dollar short," he grumbled, though it was more like two weeks.

He still had his hand on the glass when Pilar came up behind him.

"Are you going to the Harcourt mansion?"

He barely gave her a nod before pushing open the door. "Then I'm coming with you."

Outside, he turned back to her, ready to argue, but she looked so determined that he didn't bother. She'd said she wanted to do whatever she could to help him. Well, maybe he should give her the chance.

Besides, he had no idea what he would find when he reached the Harcourts' oversize house. It couldn't hurt to have someone with a psychology degree along with this search party.

He unlocked his car door, and Pilar climbed in and clicked her seat belt. Neither spoke as he pulled the car out of the station parking lot.

Maybe Ashley had run, and they wouldn't find her at all. At least not now. Wherever she was, he just wanted her to be all right.

This story wasn't the same as Jasmine's, he kept repeating in his mind. Only some mistakes ended up as tragedies. Some people got to live with the consequences of theirs. But others weren't so fortunate.

He pushed the accelerator a little harder.

# Chapter Thirteen

"Ashley," Pilar called into the kitchen door she'd opened in the cavernous Harcourt mansion. Her voice echoed off faraway walls, but the only other sounds she heard were from squirrels cracking nuts at the base of a huge maple not far from the entrance.

"Ashley, are you in here?"

She'd often wondered what the mansion would look like up close instead of from a distance atop its mile-long driveway, but this way felt like such an invasion. She had no business being here.

When Zach had hurried out of the police station to find Ashley, she'd been so sure she would be there, but she felt far less certain now. She didn't even know Ashley Harcourt except by newspaper pictures for all her school awards. How had she thought she was going to be of some help when she got there?

"Is that door unlocked?" Zach rushed around from

the back of house where he'd planned to try the pool-house entrance. "That one was locked, too."

"It doesn't sound like there's anyone in there."

He came up beside her and pushed the door all the way open. "This place is so big that a half-dozen people could be inside, and they'd barely notice each other."

Pilar followed him into the huge stainless-steel kitchen. "I guess you're right. Rachel said the house has seven bedrooms and nine bathrooms."

Together, they passed a dining room with a long mahogany table and a crystal chandelier, and then crossed through a mammoth living room that looked like a designer's showroom before they reached a grand stairway. Zach took the stairs two at time, so she rushed to keep up.

At the top, he pointed down a long hallway. "You take the east wing. I'll take the west."

She followed his direction, but she'd only entered the second empty bedroom when she heard him call out.

"Pilar, in here."

Hurrying toward where she believed she'd heard the sound, she stepped into a room decorated in lavender and pastel yellow.

"Zach, where are you?"

She scanned the room with its filmy white curtains, Victorian dollhouse in the corner and a huge lacy canopy over the four-poster bed. It was a child's room, certainly not a place where a seventeen-year-old girl would live. Still, the bedcovers were twisted, and wrappers of food items littered the nightstand, so someone had been there recently.

"In the bathroom. Hurry."

In the far corner, she noticed light leading from an open door. She could hear him talking to someone in a soft voice. She rushed to the door to find him crouched down just inside it. Beyond him, lying curled up in a blanket was a young woman she could only imagine was Ashley Harcourt. She didn't look anything like the newspaper photos. Her hair was supposed to be blond, but it was so wet with sweat that it appeared black.

"It's going to be all right, Ashley," Zach crooned to the girl as he brushed hair back from her face. "I'm Detective Fletcher and this is Pilar Estes, and we're going to get you to the hospital."

"So cold," she whispered, her teeth chattering though the blanket covered her up to her chin.

"I know you are, but we'll help you get warm again real soon," he told her.

"I think I'm going to vomit." But she didn't jerk up and reach for the toilet. One of her hands wormed out of the covers to press against her lower back. "It hurts." With the last she cried out, her eyes squeezed shut.

Zach looked over his shoulder at Pilar, uncertainty clouding his face, before he turned back to the girl and patted her shoulder. "Everything's going to be fine."

Pilar crouched beside him to lend her support. "It's okay, Ashley. Help is here now."

"I want my…"

"Mom?" Pilar filled in the word for her. Children always seemed to cry out for their mothers when they were sick, even those with mothers unworthy of that title. This poor disoriented girl probably needed her mother now more than ever.

But Ashley only shook her head so hard that her long, loose hair whipped back and forth. "Want my baby."

Pilar stilled, her breath stuck in her throat.

Zach turned and shoved his cell phone into her hand. "Here. Call an ambulance."

The phone felt cold on her skin, but for the life of her, Pilar couldn't lift her other hand to dial it. Her feet seemed to be cemented to the floor.

Zach stood and hurried to the sink, dampening a washcloth before turning back to brush it over the young woman's face.

He looked over his shoulder again. "Pilar," he said in a sharp voice. "You've got to snap out of it."

Her head jerked, and she came to her feet.

"Now try to dial."

She did as she was instructed, her thoughts no more clear than they'd been from the moment she'd seen Ashley collapsed on the floor. Somehow she even managed to give the police dispatcher the address of the Harcourt mansion before Zach reached out for her to hand him the phone.

As she released it, she glanced at the nightstand a second time. Beside it, a large wastebasket overflowed with crumpled tissues, as if the person who'd rested in the bed had suffered from a terrible cold. Or had been crying her heart out.

No, she couldn't think about those things now. About mommies and babies and how real mothers didn't leave. About mistakes and regrets and second chances. She couldn't wrap her thoughts around any of it right now. She wouldn't even let herself try.

Everything happened so quickly after that. Sirens blared. Emergency workers converged like a military invasion. A girl was taken away on a gurney. In what seemed like only minutes, the house was empty again except for Zach and Pilar, who stood near the kitchen door.

"Are you okay?" Zach asked the question, though the fact that he put his hand under her elbow to steady her suggested he already knew the answer.

A shrug was the best response she could come up with. "Do you think she'll be all right?" She couldn't shake the image of the pale, feverish teenager, crying for her baby. Her heart ached for that broken child and her family.

He shook his head. "Hard to tell. The EMTs said her blood pressure was dangerously low. I don't know what that means."

His grim expression and creased forehead suggested that he'd at least guessed. If Ashley died, would Zach be forced to live his sister's death all over again? For a few seconds he squeezed his eyes shut and pinched the bridge of his nose as if he was fighting off a headache. He was reliving Jasmine's death, all right.

"You did the best you could."

Zach opened his eyes and glanced sidelong at her.

"Did I?" He paused, probably turning his recrimination inward. "Do you think the Harcourts or their daughter will think so?" His words came out like the acid he must have been feeling inside.

But Pilar couldn't let him do this, not when he'd turned himself inside out looking for clues to lead them to Gabriel's mother. Plenty of mistakes had been made in Ashley Harcourt's unfortunate situation, and she refused to let Zach take the blame for all of them. He'd already accepted more blame than anyone should in one lifetime.

"Just give yourself a break, will you?" She let out an exasperated sigh. "You probably saved her life."

"And if I didn't?"

Their gazes met, but neither spoke since there was no good answer to that question. In silence, they climbed in his car and turned back toward the station.

Pilar risked a glance at him, but his gaze was focused on the road, his jaw tight. The situation just didn't seem fair. Though he worked in the criminal justice system, there'd been no justice for Zach. He'd found the answers to close this case, but the answers brought him not relief but a chance to relive his darkest days. If only there was something she could do to help him.

*Father, please provide healing in this situation for Ashley and her family. And, Lord, help Zach to find peace with his past and present.*

Mouthing the word "amen," Pilar felt her stomach clench with uncertainty. She sent out one last desperate appeal: *Please let her live.*

She should have been asking for God's will in the situation, so she hoped He would understand. This wasn't for her but for the man she loved, the man who'd already lost too much. Though the whole situation was plagued with uncertainties, there was one thing she felt certain about: If they were already too late and Ashley died, Zach would never forgive himself.

Zach couldn't tell if the antiseptic odor in his nostrils was real or simply part of a memory he was fighting to block out as he waited at the Bon Secours Richmond Community Hospital late Monday night. Still, he swallowed hard to keep from gagging at the smell while the grim news played over and over in his mind like an old record, its music discordant, its lyrics interminable.

Septicemia, they'd called her condition. The E.R. doctor had surmised that it started with a simple bladder infection from the delivery and had continued over days unchecked into a kidney infection. Left untreated in those thirteen days since Gabriel's birth, the bacteria had spread through her whole body, causing the pain, the chills and what else he didn't even want to imagine.

The doctors had told him they were fortunate they'd gotten to her before her organs began to shut down. Somehow he didn't feel very fortunate.

Though he hadn't seen her since the ambulance pulled away, he could still picture Ashley, lying curled up on the bathroom floor, delirious with fever. So quickly her image transformed from damp blond hair and dark eyes to the long wavy tresses and deep blue eyes that would haunt his thoughts for as long as he lived.

Had history gone ahead and repeated itself no matter how hard he'd tried to prevent it? Would another family bear the pain and the blame of a lost life? Why hadn't he been able to stop it?

He shook his head hard to expel the images and the feeling that he'd failed Jasmine all over again. No, the circumstances weren't the same as the other at all. Ashley was still in there fighting to survive. The doctors were battling the infection with hydrating fluids and IV antibiotics. God willing, this young woman might even have the opportunity to grow up and face the consequences of her mistakes instead of losing her life to them.

"Any word from the doctors?"

Glancing up from the floor, he saw two cups of vending machine coffee first, and then Pilar stretching out one of them to him.

He shook his head. "Not in the last five minutes." Other than a few short breaks like that one, they'd both been keeping vigil in the intensive care unit waiting room all night. His sergeant would call this going beyond the call of duty, but his shift was long since over, so it was up to him whether or not he chose to hang out at the hospital, waiting for word. That Pilar had stayed with him meant more than he could say.

Her mouth curved in a sad smile. "I could hope, couldn't I? I'm just waiting for God to heal her."

Zach made his best attempt at a smile. She was trying; he could, too. He accepted the coffee and held it between his hands for several seconds, letting the warmth seep through his fingers, before taking a sip. He should have been numb to it by now, but it tasted just as nasty as the last two cups.

"Any word on the Harcourts?"

Pilar took a drink from her cup and grimaced. "Rachel said their flight was to take off from London two hours ago, so they'll make it in by morning."

Neither of them bothered to point out that it was almost morning already. Ashley had already held on quite a while. Now she just had to keep fighting through that first critical twenty-four hours.

"The sergeant has assigned a squad car to meet them at the Richmond airport."

She nodded, still standing there. With purple half-moons shadowing her eyes, she looked as if she could sleep without bothering to lie down.

"Here. Sit." He patted the seat next to his.

She dropped into the seat with a sigh. When Zach put his arm around her shoulders, she snuggled into the crook of his arm.

"This is nice," she murmured, her eyes closed.

"There's nothing else we can do for a while. Why don't you try to rest?"

She looked up at him from under her lashes. "Are you sure everything's okay here?"

He couldn't help smiling, knowing full well he was the *everything* she spoke of. "Sure, everything will be fine."

"I guess it will be a while before the Harcourts get here. I could rest my eyes for a few minutes."

At least one of them would get some shut-eye because he probably couldn't, at least until he knew his suspect was going to be all right. Only a few minutes after Pilar lowered her eyelids, her breathing steadied in sleep. Her long lashes were still and her facial muscles calmed.

Even as she snuggled deeper into his shoulder, Zach continued watching her sleep. She probably would have frowned if she'd seen herself in the mirror with her skin wiped free of cosmetics and her braid rumpled from resting her head on the back of the uncomfortable waiting room chair. But he couldn't remember a time when she'd looked more beautiful.

All day she had stayed there waiting with him, praying with him and consuming unimaginable amounts of liquid-tar coffee with him. She'd been strong for him on a day when he'd felt helpless. She'd stayed silent when he needed her to, talked with him when he was ready and simply let him know that she was there and she intended to stay put.

If he hadn't already fallen in love with Pilar, after today, he would have taken a swan dive of his own free will. What had he ever done to deserve such an amazing gift from God? She was everything he'd never known he wanted and everything only the Father could have known he needed. She made him believe in himself and believe that loving her was worth the risk of hurt.

Pilar shifted again in her sleep before settling against

his shoulder once more. After her breathing steadied again, Zach rested his head against hers. For the first time all day, he finally could relax, even if sleep was out of the question. No matter how dark the day had been, he had the sense now that everything was going to be all right.

Voices all around her caused Pilar to awaken with a start that sent her crashing into something hard. Rubbing the side of her throbbing head, she turned to see Zach doing the same thing. He shook his head, a pained expression on his face.

"Wake up, sleepyhead," Rachel called from across the waiting room where she stood with her fiancé, Eli Cavanaugh.

Pilar glanced at Zach and back at Rachel, feeling her cheeks grow warm, but her friend didn't seem to notice.

"Come on, guys," Eli called to them. "It's good news."

Rachel pointed down the hall to where a woman with short blond hair and a man with tan skin and dark hair stood talking to Dr. Rebecca Niles, the E.R. doctor who'd been treating Ashley. The woman that Pilar assumed to be Helene Harcourt threw herself into her husband's arms and sobbed.

"Good news?" Zach asked as he scrambled out of his seat and rushed down the hall.

Pilar followed close behind him. When he reached the couple, Zach shot out his hand.

"Are you the Harcourts? I'm Detective Zach Fletcher."

"Then you're the man who saved our daughter's life." Helene turned and hugged Zach, another sob escaping her.

Zach eyes were wide when he glanced sidelong at Pilar.

After several seconds, Neal gently pulled his wife away but wrapped a securing arm around her shoulder.

Zach looked back and forth between the couple and the doctor. "What are you saying?"

Dr. Niles answered for all of them. "Ashley's no longer hypotensive, meaning her blood pressure is returning to the normal range. Her fever is starting to come down, as is her elevated white blood cell count. All of these signs are encouraging."

"The good doctor's saying our baby girl's going to be okay." Neal didn't even fight them as twin tears trailed down his cheeks.

"Thank God for that," Helene said quietly.

The woman looked up and shared a private exchange with her husband. Tears glistened in Helene's eyes again.

Rachel looked at the couple with a quizzical expression. "Something's changed, hasn't it?"

"We had a long flight back from London and an awful lot of talking to do," Neal explained.

"We've messed things up so badly. We've been this close to divorce for the last five years." Helene indicated an inch with her forefinger and thumb. "Our daughter Samantha's been in and out of treatment for anorexia for years."

"And now Ashley. When we think about what we

could have lost today because our daughter couldn't come to us…" Neal finished for his wife but let his words trail off, too choked up to continue.

Helene picked up the story. "We figured it was time—way past time—for us to turn our lives over to the only one who can make them right. We want to become the family we should have been all along. We have a marriage, two daughters and now a grandson to protect."

Again, the couple exchanged a private glance.

"Oh, I'm so glad."

At the sound of the voice behind them, those in the room turned to see Beatrice Noble rush through the doorway. She headed straight to her friends and hugged them both at the same time.

"Our Lord can make it right. You believe that, okay?" Beatrice gave each of them an extra squeeze before she released them.

Helene took her friend's hand. "We're going to do whatever we can to help Ashley and her baby. Whatever she needs."

"You let us know if you need anything, too, okay?" Beatrice said.

Neal reached over and messed up Beatrice's spiky hair. "You already did a lot by slipping that tract about salvation into my wife's carry-on."

Beatrice only raised an eyebrow. "Who, me?" Then she winked. "I knew it would come in handy one day."

Rachel moved closer to her mother then and put an

arm around her shoulder. "Sounds as if great things are happening to several of our friends lately." She looked pointedly at Zach and Pilar. Zach coughed into his hand and turned away, likely feeling as awkward at Pilar did.

Her friend probably would have said more, but a nurse came out of the door that led to the ICU and approached the doctor. They spoke to each other in hushed tones.

When Dr. Niles turned back to the Harcourts, she was grinning. "Ashley is awake now. She's asking to speak to the both of you."

Zach stepped forward. "I'll also need to take a statement from her as soon as possible."

The doctor held up a hand but nodded at the same time. "Of course, Detective. But first I think our patient needs some time with her parents."

## Chapter Fourteen

Just as before, Zach and Pilar were suddenly alone in the waiting room as the Harcourts attended to their daughter and the doctor and their other friends returned to their duties and lives. They even returned to the same chairs, where Zach had let Pilar rest with her head on his shoulder.

But other than location, nothing about the situation was the same.

"How do family relationships like that ever get so far gone?" Pilar pondered aloud as she stretched her arms above her head.

"I'm probably not the best person to ask that question."

"Probably not," she agreed. "That's great that both of them made their professions of faith."

He nodded. "A lot of great things happened today. I can't believe she's going to be all right."

"Did you ever doubt it?"

He only rolled his eyes. "You know, I covet you your faith sometimes."

"Doesn't coveting fall under those Ten Commandments we always read about? You're not supposed to covet your neighbor's house or butler or his ox or anything. I think that includes his faith."

He shook his head, but he couldn't keep from smiling. "Okay then. Can I just be amazed by you?"

She opened her mouth, probably to spout a funny comeback, but then she clicked her teeth shut. She bit her lower lip and stared at the ground.

"I am, you know," he continued. "You see the good in people even when it's not all that easy to see without a microscope. You trust people. You'd do anything for anybody without ever thinking about yourself."

Pilar licked her lips. "You do things for people, too. Just look at the lengths you went to in order to find Gabriel's mother."

"I love those things about you," he continued, not letting her change the subject.

She glanced up at him and flashed an embarrassed smile before looking at her toes again.

"You came here for me. You stayed. You wanted to make things easier on me even though none of it—about the baby—could be easy for you right now."

She shrugged. "I'm okay. Really. I just wanted to help because I could only guess what memories were going through your mind—"

"I thought she was going to die, but you never questioned whether she would be okay. You stuck around and gave me hope when I didn't have any."

She held her hands wide. "That's what friends are for. You did the same for me right after the surgery—"

He put up his hand to interrupt her. She was pushing the conversation away from things he wanted to say. Things he had to say now before he lost his courage.

"I love you, Pilar."

For several seconds, she sat still. Too still. He held his breath. Even after all they'd been through together he worried that she would rebuff his declaration. That she would tell him she'd only reached out to him because she sensed he needed a friend. But then slowly she looked up at him, tears shining in her eyes.

"Do you know how long I've waited for you to say those words?"

She wasn't making any sense. His profession had come at breakneck speed as far as he was concerned. "What do you mean?"

Pilar smiled. "From probably the first time I met you, I saw all of these wonderful qualities in you. I wanted you to see me, but you didn't."

He shook his head and clasped her hand in his. Somehow, he had to make her understand. "No, that's not it. I didn't *want* to see you. I didn't want to let anybody in."

"Are you sorry you did?"

Was he? He tilted his head, considering. But every misgiving fled on a surge of confidence. "Never." Then because the words, once spoken, clamored to be repeated, he said it once more. "I love you."

"I love you, too."

Though medical professionals in blue scrubs passed in and out of the room and buzzers and beeps of medical equipment serenaded them, it felt as if the two of them were the only ones in the hospital.

Zach lifted her hand and studied it, tracing his fingers along the curves of her palm. Her hand curled over his, and soon their fingers had laced in a connection that bespoke a permanence that he was only beginning to recognize he'd always wanted.

With his other hand, he tilted her chin and brushed his lips across hers. It was a kiss of commitment. His heart was there for her to take. He held nothing back this time. He'd wasted so much energy in his life running from people who cared about him, and now all he wanted to do was stick where he was and to focus all that energy on loving Pilar.

Zach knocked and waited outside the semi-private room where Ashley Harcourt had been moved a half hour before.

"Yes," a small voice called from inside.

He pushed open the door. A young woman who looked nothing like the girl he'd found lying in her bathroom sat propped in a railed hospital bed. Her hair wasn't sweaty and matted but had been combed until it shone and carefully plaited on both sides to just below her collarbones. Probably her mother's work. She looked very much the little girl he suspected she still was in many ways.

"Ashley, I'm Detective Fletcher."

"I know who you are. I remember your voice. You told me it was going to be okay." She paused for several seconds, studying him. "You were right."

He coughed into his hand, surprised at the emotions wound up by her words.

"It was good that we found you when we did." He refused to let himself shudder at the thought of them arriving even one day later.

"Thanks. You saved my life."

"A lot of people were involved."

"Thank them, too, will you?"

He nodded. "I have to ask you some questions about the events of September the first."

Immediately, her eyes glazed with tears. "The day I abandoned my baby. The day I'll regret as long as I live."

Zach took the seat next to her bed and rested his hand on hers. "I know this is painful, but I need to know what really happened, and you're the only one who can tell me."

But Ashley didn't seem to be listening. She stared out the window at the gray fall day, a sad smile pulling on her lips.

"He was so sweet, just resting there in his little basket, trusting me to do the right thing. I was his mommy. I had to do what was best for him.

"It couldn't matter that it hurt me so much I nearly forgot how to breathe the minute I left him on that porch. I watched for five minutes from down the street until Pilar came to work—early like usual."

Zach took notes as Ashley told her story, not nearly as clear-cut as it would have appeared from the initial report. Personal tragedies like that never were. What had begun as a teenager acting out after the mysterious death of the grandfather she adored had led to a situation that had spiraled out of control.

Jasmine had probably felt the same way after her first mistake had led to another, and then another to cover that one. If only someone had been there to listen to his sister's story, to offer compassion. That was the past, he reminded himself, and there wasn't anything he could do to change it. But he could play a role here, and he wanted to play it the best he could.

"I love my baby, Detective. I just knew my parents would never accept him." She shook her head, tears she'd been holding back finally spilling from her eyes. "Look at me. I'm still a kid. I knew without my parents' support, I'd never be able to give Gabriel a good home. The kind of home he deserves."

He nodded. If only there were more parents—young or old—who put their children's needs before their own.

"Do you know the identity of the baby's father?" He made a point of looking at his notes after asking the necessary but very personal question.

"Yes, but I won't tell since I never want any contact from him. He's from Richmond, so no one knows him here." She met his gaze squarely when he looked up at her. "No one would want to."

The interview flowed easily after that, though the answers still fell in that void between the law and the actions of a desperate young woman. There was no clear black and white, only more shades of gray than anyone dared enumerate. His own job didn't leave any room for those varying shades, so he could only hope that someone with more authority than he had could step in and help make things right.

"You have a guest," Kelly said as she passed Pilar's desk on the way to her office Tuesday afternoon.

Because Kelly hadn't bothered to hide her grin, Pilar didn't have to wonder who was waiting for her in Tiny Blessings' reception area. As she stood up from her desk, her pulse tripped at just the thought of seeing Zach again. He loved her. He'd said it twice. For the next thirty years, he could say it twice a day, and she would never tire of hearing it.

"Hi, there." Zach hadn't even bothered to sit in one of the reception area chairs, but was standing and waiting for her.

"Hi, yourself."

He looked wonderful in a honey-brown polo shirt and tan trousers, an upgrade from his usual rumpled look, but that would have been fine, too. She'd been missing him from the moment he dropped her off at her apartment four hours before.

Without hesitating, Zach crossed the reception area and rested his hands on her shoulders, lowering his head to kiss her hello. He hadn't even bothered to check first to see if anyone else was nearby. Just as he pulled away, Anne scurried from the room, looking embarrassed. Far from contrite, Zach grinned.

"I'll be outside if you need me," Pilar called after her, unable to contain her nervous titter.

They descended the building's back steps and followed the walk to the courtyard, sitting on the edge of the granite fountain that had been turned off for the season. Though gold-and-red leaves dotted the small lawn, enclosed by ivy-wrapped wrought iron, Pilar couldn't remember the grounds ever looking more beautiful. Even the sky appeared bluer now that he was there with her.

Zach was still grinning as he took her hand.

"Well, you're in a wonderful mood today. Is there more good news on Ashley's recovery?"

"The best."

When he didn't elaborate immediately, she pressed, "What's the news?"

"She's out of the ICU, and she might even get to go home tomorrow."

"Praise God for that. Ashley's got a long road ahead of her, though, as she and her parents rebuild their relationship. They'll need to work on finding a good counselor right away."

"They'll also need to get the nursery decorated."

Pilar withdrew her hand and shook her head, certain she hadn't heard him right. "Excuse me?"

He glanced at his empty hand for a second before he met her gaze again. "That's the other great news. Ashley wants to keep Gabriel, and her parents are supporting her decision."

If he'd smacked her with a baseball bat to the calves, her knees wouldn't have buckled more quickly. "What—" She'd spoken louder than she'd planned, so she started again in a lower tone. "What are you talking about?"

He beamed as if he'd just given her the best news ever. "I finally got in to interview her about an hour ago. We talked about a lot of things, not just the investigation."

He paused for so long that Pilar was convinced she would implode if he didn't tell her everything that instant.

Zach nodded, looking as if he was in agreement with whatever thought had just passed through his mind. "There will be court hearings and ultimately a judge's decision, but Ashley wants to be a mother to her son."

She came so quickly to her feet that her head swam. "Are you kidding?"

He drew his eyebrows together as he looked up at her. "Why would I kid about that?"

"What about the criminal charges Ashley's facing for *abandoning* her son?"

She couldn't help putting extra emphasis on "abandoning" because Zach seemed to have forgotten that the girl had done anything more severe than to show up late to pick up her baby from the babysitter.

He cocked his head to the side and studied her before speaking again. "That's not my area. I only gather evidence for court cases. But I'm guessing that the court might be lenient here, especially since Ashley now has the support of her family."

"Some family," she muttered.

Stiffening this time, Zach gripped the edge of the fountain seat beneath him. His glare was filled with warning. "They're not perfect, but they're trying. Ashley's sister, Samantha, is even moving home from D.C. to be with her. They're registering for counseling—just like you recommended—because they want to make their family the best place for Gabriel to grow up."

Pilar shot her hand out to dismiss the idea. "So Gabriel gets to be the test case to see if their grand plan for reuniting their family is working?"

Zach came to his feet and faced her. "What are *you* talking about? Where is this coming from?" His arms were crossed, his jaw tight.

She hated that he was angry with her, but this was too important for her to back down. "Zach, she deserted her baby." She spread her arms wide and enunciated each word to make her point.

"She rested him on her parents' fancy cashmere blanket in her family's heirloom picnic basket and dumped him on the adoption agency's doorstep like he was nothing."

Zach shook his head, his crossed arms tightening. "I

shouldn't have to explain this to someone with your professional background, but have you ever heard of extenuating circumstances? She's not even eighteen yet. Without her parents' support, she'd never be able to provide for her baby, and she was afraid they would never accept him."

"That didn't give her any excuse to abandon him."

"No, it didn't, but it gave her a reason. I believe she loves her baby and wanted to do the right thing for him—even if, ultimately, it wasn't the right thing. That's why I'm going to testify on her behalf in court."

"How can you do that?" The words were out of her mouth before she could stop them. She'd gone too far and she knew it, but still she couldn't help but say more. "How can you say what she did is okay? She left her newborn outside. He could have *died*. Don't you see that she's unfit to be Gabriel's mother?"

"Who are you to decide that? I thought that was the judge's job."

Pilar flinched. "How do you know that the next time things get tough—like when he's teething or in the terrible twos—that she won't drop him off at the mall or any other place she can find?"

Zach stalked away from her to the fence, where he gripped two of the black bars, clearly trying to regain control of his emotions. Finally, he faced her.

"That's not fair, and you know it. You saw her note. She wanted her baby to be placed with a loving family."

"This isn't about fair." She planted her hands on her waist. "It's about Gabriel."

"Is it? Tell me, Pilar, is it really about Gabriel, or is this whole thing about you? Is it about a fantasy that the court would have the great idea of making you Gabriel's mother?"

She jerked at the sting of his words. He hadn't even said it, but she knew he was really asking if it was about her fears that she would never have children. She shook her head hard to dispel that thought and all of his mistaken assumptions.

"That's not it." She opened her hands wide. Somehow she had to make him understand. "This is just like what you said about some things you can never take back. No matter how many pretty excuses she comes up with, Ashley *left* her baby. She can never change that. Anyone who abandons her child doesn't deserve a second chance."

For several long seconds, Zach just stared at her, his eyes wide. Then he started shaking his head as if he was having an argument with himself and losing. He pointed his index finger at her. "Who are you?"

Her breath caught in her throat as the subtext of the conversation dawned on her. It had been more than about Ashley all along, and she'd trampled in verbal combat boots all over the subject—and his memories of his sister.

"Zach, I…" She wasn't sure what to say, but it was pointless anyway because he only walked away from her.

He stopped and looked back at her, his expression vague as if he was looking at a stranger. "How could I have been so wrong about you? I thought you were compassionate. I thought you cared about people."

Slowly, Pilar came up behind him, but not too close for fear he would only stalk away again. "I do care. You know that." If that was true, then why did her words ring so empty in her ears?

"You're just like them."

Again, she flinched. She didn't want to be grouped among the "them" that he didn't even have to identify for her to know: his parents.

"I'm not," she said in a weak voice.

He acted as if he didn't hear her. "You're just as judgmental and unforgiving as they were."

"You're wrong." She shook her head again, though a seed of uncertainty sprouted inside her.

"*They* were wrong, all right." He turned to face her. "The price of their mistake was high—two lives."

Dread sank low in her gut as she realized she would pay a high cost, as well. She was losing the only man she had ever, and probably would ever, love. She felt him slipping through her fingers like grains of sand on a windy beach, not just fluttering to the ground but scattering in all directions.

As if he only now realized that their argument had taken place in the courtyard and that others might have overheard, Zach lowered his voice. "I was right about you all along. I knew better. You were too perfect."

"What do you mean, perfect?" Her question came as a whisper because she'd never felt more flawed.

"You told me that I hadn't seemed to see you when we first met. Oh, I saw you, all right. I saw your perfect, intact family and your perfect life."

He glanced at her quickly and then looked away again. "You were so beautiful that I didn't want to come anywhere near you for fear that my muddled-up life would mar all that perfection."

She swallowed hard and her eyes filled. Her chest ached so badly that it felt as if someone had laid a weight over her and left her there, struggling to breathe. His revelation answered so many questions but only left her raw inside. He'd thought her beautiful then, but had found her unapproachable. Now he knew her as well as anyone, and he didn't want to be anywhere near her.

"Please, Zach, you know me now. I'm not perfect. I never said I was." Tears flowed freely down her cheeks, and she didn't even bother to brush them away. "Maybe I overreacted about Ashley's situation. Maybe I'm too close to the subject. Maybe we both are."

"There is no *we*." Turning away, he started toward his car.

"But Zach," Pilar called after him, "you said…you said…you loved me."

He stopped. Hope and doom battled inside her as she watched him, so still on the outside when a war as confusing as her own likely waged within him. Finally, he turned back to her, his expression blank.

"It doesn't matter what I said. I can't be with you. I can't be with someone who doesn't know how to forgive."

Without looking back, he continued to his car, climbed in and drove away. A sob escaped her throat as Pilar sank back on the seat at the fountain's edge and buried her face in her hands. Her fingers felt wet, her insides numb.

*You're just like them.*

His words accused her. Delivered a strong prosecution with no defense. So she stayed there and cried, not feeling the cool air swirling around her. She closed her eyes, but there didn't seem to be any way to block out the truth and the conviction in her heart: He was right.

# *Chapter Fifteen*

"Hold on there, buddy," Zach called through the front door as he unlocked his apartment. Already, whimpers and scratching came from the other side of the door.

Turning the knob, he braced himself for Rudy's seventy-pound greeting. The dog didn't disappoint, and Zach wiped his wet chin, giving his pet a good scratching behind the ears. Without turning on the light, he reached inside and retrieved the dog's leash and a small trash bag from their regular spots on a stack of boxes.

He frowned into the darkness as he snapped the retractable leash onto the German shepherd's collar. "How can you bear to live with me?"

But Rudy didn't fill him in on the challenges that went with being Detective Zach Fletcher's roommate. Instead, he danced around the hallway and announced his need for an immediate bathroom break with a sharp bark.

"Hush, boy. Do you want to get us evicted?" But

Zach let the dog lead him out the door and into the complex's commons area.

Outside, he glanced up at his darkened apartment window and frowned again. Why did he suddenly resent the place that had served him and his dog well for the last two years? Probably because today he took exception to nearly everything in his life, himself most of all.

As soon as Rudy was ready, Zach returned to the apartment, but his sour mood came back inside with him. He wished he could have shed it as easily he had his jacket, which he'd tossed on another box along the wall. Even the dog must have noticed that something wasn't right with him because Rudy nuzzled his hand and paced through the apartment, as unsettled as his owner.

Zach tried to shake off his funk by getting on with his nighttime routine, but when he flipped the light switch, it only illuminated just how empty his apartment was. His life was. The hand-me-down chipped dishes and the bare walls he'd never paid attention to before mocked him now.

Boxes he'd packed for his move from Philadelphia still lined the walls, used now for storage instead of transport. Couldn't he at least have nailed up a single framed print in more than two years? Maybe one of those cheesy nature-scene calendars?

No wonder he'd never brought Pilar to see his place, though he'd seen plenty of hers while she recuperated. If it weren't for the books stacked by the leather couch, the always-current television guide by the remote and an open box of cereal on the kitchen counter, the place would look vacant. Nothing there, other than a few chew toys and a sprinkling of dog fur, made it feel like home.

Like Pilar's apartment. He'd felt more at home there than he'd ever felt inside his own four walls—the same walls that seemed to close in around him while he paced the room.

He wondered what she was doing at home right then. Had she already eaten her dinner at her tiny dinette? Was she relaxing on her sofa, watching television or reading? Had she spent some time breathing in the cool evening air while sitting on her balcony?

So easily he could picture her in any of those places, and he smiled at the image they brought to his mind. But the image changed, and so did his thoughts. Had she spent the evening crying instead because of him?

He didn't want to believe it, but he'd seen the first of those tears before he'd even left the courtyard outside her office. Were there more later? He wanted to shout to her, to tell her he wasn't worth crying over, and yet his own eyes burned.

Running from those thoughts, Zach stalked across the living room/dining room that was far bigger than the one in Pilar's apartment, and hoisted a bag of what manufacturers would have more accurately called "horse chow." He filled Rudy's bowl, and the dog didn't waste any time digging in, his dinner late for the third time in as many days.

"Sorry you had to wait, buddy."

He grabbed the water bowl and refilled it in the

kitchen sink, but the dog was still crunching contentedly when he returned.

"At least one of us has something to be happy about."

For the apartment's other occupant, prospects for happiness were pretty much nil after the things he'd said today. *I can't be with someone who doesn't know how to forgive.* Even if she did know how, which in his heart he knew she did, she probably would choose not to use that ability for his sake. He certainly didn't deserve one of those second chances they'd argued about.

A person who loved someone didn't speak to her that way, even when he believed she was wrong. And he still did believe she was wrong, but his accusing her had been like calling the kettle not only black, but black and hot and whistling.

She could have told him that. She could have called him the hypocrite he was for focusing on her, when he should have been looking inward. But she hadn't. She'd just taken everything he'd dished out and let it convict her.

Though he'd been only a child in Sunday school when he'd memorized the verse, Jesus' words in the Book of Matthew filtered into his thoughts then. *Why do you see the speck that is in your brother's eye, but do not notice the log that is in your own eye?*

How long had he been carrying the weight of that log? When would he finally have the courage to remove it? What could he do to fix the mess he'd made of his relationship with Pilar? Could he get the do-over he didn't deserve, or was it something he couldn't take back?

Zach sat on his sofa and dropped his head into his hands, the weight of the questions heavy on his shoulders. But inside him the agitation only multiplied. He couldn't stay there anymore. He had to get out of there before those bare walls folded in on him.

Leaping up, he patted his startled dog on the head and grabbed his jacket. He didn't even bother to shut off the light. He'd spent too much of his life in the darkness of blame and doubt, anyway.

He hurried out to his car and climbed in. Turning the ignition, he drove into the night, heading for the one place where he was convinced he would find peace.

Pilar glanced at the clock on her dashboard as she pulled her car into the spot nearest her church's side entrance. It was nearly 11:30 p.m. Reverend Fraser had always had a policy of leaving the small side door unlocked all night for anyone needing to enter the sanctuary to pray. She only hoped that the vandalism and fire at the adoption agency hadn't made him amend that policy because she really needed some time in prayer tonight.

Not that she had to do it inside the church—she knew God listened wherever she talked to Him. But she had the feeling they would be having a long discussion, and she'd always felt closer to God while she rested on one of the aged wood pews and prayed open-eyed while staring out the stained-glass windows.

Tonight, though, she would close her eyes since the sun wouldn't be there to illuminate the glass scenes of the Cross and the words of Jesus' commission to "Go ye therefore, and teach all nations."

"I'm here, Father," she whispered even before she opened the door.

Why she felt the need to move silently, she didn't know. The building would be empty at this hour. Even Reverend Fraser didn't work this late—not if Naomi had anything to say about it. Still, Pilar pulled open the glass door with great care and closed it behind her.

Her heart was so heavy after a day of the Lord convicting her. Zach had been right about her. Where was her compassion for Ashley and her son? She'd been thinking only of herself, of her own fears, not that child, not that mother. She'd hated seeing the girl regain custody when others would have given anything to have a child.

What room did her judgment leave for second chances like those God had so freely given her? How had she shown Christ's love to the "least of these," while she was refusing to forgive a young woman who'd made a terrible mistake?

She'd been selfish and self-centered today just as she'd been every day since she found out about her fertility issues. Her selfishness had not only lost her the earthly man she loved, but it had cost her a right relationship with her Lord, and she couldn't bear that. And wouldn't any longer.

The first thing that struck her as she started down the aisle was a small light in the sanctuary. Coming from behind the baptismal, it bathed the pews and the altar in soft yellow light. Pilar stopped and stared. She understood that where two or three gathered, the Lord promised to be in their midst, but still she felt His presence there, as well—in the silence.

Reverently, she continued toward the altar, but when she'd made it halfway, she stopped cold. She wasn't alone there after all. Zach was kneeling on the steps at the base of the altar.

Her heart squeezed in misery from being so close and yet so far from him, but she turned to go anyway. His prayer time was private. He hadn't come here to have an audience but to be alone with his God just as she'd planned to do. But he started praying aloud then, and she felt weighted into place, an eavesdropper to a spiritual conversation.

"Lord, please help me to finally let go of my anger, to finally forgive."

Her breath caught in her throat. Her eyes and nose burned, predicting tears that weren't far behind. Even if she couldn't have Zach in her life, she wanted him to finally make peace with his past. Maybe even to heal that chasm between himself and his parents. She wanted that because she loved him more than she needed to be with him.

"And Lord," Zach began again, "help me find a way to earn her forgiveness. Help me to show her that I love her…without conditions."

Whether it was a sob or a gasp that escaped her throat, she wasn't sure, but whatever it was, the sound brought Zach's head up from his folded hands. She knew the minute he recognized her from the shadows, because his body stilled.

"I'm sorry. I didn't mean to—" She started backing away, not sure what to do, but then she stopped herself. Mustering all the courage she could, she strode purposely down the aisle to him.

He stood and faced her when she reached him.

"Zach, I'm so sorry. I was wrong—"

But he raised a hand to stop her. Her heart squeezed. Had she misunderstood what he'd said? Was she lying to herself to believe that she could be at peace if Zach finally found healing, but still chose not to be with her? Would the pain be more than she could bear?

Zach only shook his head, his eyes too shiny. "No, I was wrong. I accused you of being unable to forgive when I was the one who never forgave my parents or myself. I went chasing after Gabriel's missing mother to prove that I could make things right for a family, even if it wasn't my own. I thought I owed it to Jasmine."

She opened her mouth, wanting to say something, anything to lessen his pain, but he shook his head. He wasn't finished.

"But I didn't make it right. Only God can do that. And if there's any relationship I need to seek His help on, it's the one with Will and Carol Fletcher of Philadelphia." He indicated his surroundings with a slow wave of his hand. "I figured I'd get started here. I have a lot of praying to do. I like to come here to pray because God feels so close here."

She glanced around again at the backlit sanctuary. "I have some praying to do myself—for forgiveness. Jesus said the world would know we were Christians by our love for other people. Nobody around today would ever accuse me of being a believer."

Zach hated to see her hurting this way. He wished he could protect her so that she never had to cry again. But because he couldn't, he took her by the hand and led her to the front pew. Taking a seat beside her, he placed his forefinger under her chin and tilted it up so she would meet his gaze and see that he was being sincere.

"How could anyone not know that you're a Christian? You of all people."

She lifted a shoulder and let it fall. "Anyone who was within listening distance of the courtyard today would have their doubts."

Because she was probably right about that, he only shrugged.

Pilar placed her elbows on her jean-clad knees and hung her head dejectedly between her fists. "I was everything you said I was. Judgmental. Unforgiving. Selfish—you didn't say the last, but it's true, too."

Zach shook his head harder with each negative adjective she used to describe herself. "You're none of those things. You're good and kind and caring."

He stopped himself then, knowing full well he could go on touting her amazing qualities until she begged him to stop. With a grin, he added, "You just lost sight of who you really were for a while."

"I really am sorry, Zach."

"No more sorry than I am. Can you forgive me? Is there a second chance?"

"Seconds. Thirds. Whatever it takes."

Pilar threw her arms around his neck, nuzzling her nose against his ear. As his arms closed around her, Zach knew he'd received the most amazing gift. A do-over. And this time he'd get it right.

When Pilar pulled away at last, she was smiling through her tears. "We really are a pair, aren't we?"

He grinned back, the conversation sounding familiar, so he answered as he had before. "Yes…we are."

But then he thought of a subject so contentious that it had rocked their barely formed foundation. As much as he hated to bring it up again and risk another tremor, he had to know the truth.

"I'm still going to testify on Ashley's behalf, you know." She started to interrupt, but he lifted his hand to make her wait.

"I have to do it. It's the right thing. Not because of my sister and my baggage that I never should have brought to this case, but because this young woman loves her baby. She's made mistakes, but she wants to do the right thing, and she deserves a second chance to be Gabriel's mother."

He waited. His breath felt tight in his chest. Wanting for things to be right on the surface between himself and

Pilar wasn't enough. There had to be a deeper under-standing between them—a respect for their different positions, even if they couldn't agree.

Pilar nodded, the smile never leaving her lips or her eyes. "I'll be right there with you. Ashley's going to need all of us to love and support her and her child. Whatever she needs…"

When she let her words trail away, Zach studied her face. She was sincere and appeared as committed as he was.

So this was what it felt like to be content. He liked it. He was pretty sure he could go on feeling this way for the long haul and never find a reason to complain.

He felt connected to Pilar on a different level as they served the Father's will together. It felt good. It felt right. It felt as if a whole other chapter of his life was opening without footnotes of earlier chapters cluttering up the pages.

Glancing around the softly lit sanctuary, Zach's gaze fell on the altar. An idea formed immediately, and he stood. "Come here."

He reached out a hand to her and waited until she curled her fingers inside his. He led her to the steps beside the altar and knelt in the same place where he'd been praying when she'd arrived. She joined him on her knees, seeming to understand without words that he wanted them to pray together.

But as he started to lead the prayer as he'd planned, her soft, melodic voice broke the silence. "Father, You know the troubles in our hearts. Our hurts. Our fears. Please give us the strength to trust You with all of them. And Lord, let us be Your eyes and Your hands here on Earth. Direct us as we try to do Your work and to follow Your will. Amen."

Zach opened his eyes and stared at her, amazed that she'd prayed for so many of the same things laying on his heart. He wanted to do God's work, and he wanted to do it with Pilar at his side.

Because he couldn't imagine his life any other way, he turned to face her as she straightened and turned to sit on the step. He scooted until he was a step lower and continued kneeling. When he lifted her hand, she tilted her head and looked at him with a confused expression.

His pulse raced and his hand became clammy, but he forced the words to come whatever way they could.

"Pilar, I'm in love with you." He squeezed her hand and could feel her trembling as much as he was inside. "I want to build a family with you."

Immediately, her eyes filled and she turned her head away from him. Didn't she understand that there were some things any couple didn't know, couldn't know as they built a life together?

"It doesn't matter. Don't you see that?" The important thing was for them to be together, but she clearly wasn't ready to believe that. He would show her every day, if only she gave him the chance.

Two fine lines of tears spilled over and trailed down

her cheeks. "But you know going in with me that there's a risk—"

"Love is a risk, sweetheart. Marriage is a risk. But it's also a decision, and I have decided to love you for the rest of my life."

"Marriage. Marriage." She rolled the word on her tongue, trying it on, seeing if it fit.

He grinned. "Has a nice ring to it, doesn't it?"

But she wasn't laughing. She stared at him. "It really doesn't matter to you."

"No, it doesn't. I love you. I choose you. The rest is up to God."

"Up to God," she repeated, but then her smile faltered. "But what if—"

"I promise you this—our home will be filled with children, whether those we make together or those we choose to love." He reached up and brushed his fingers through her hair that she'd worn loose down her back. "You probably even know a good Christian adoption agency we could work with."

She grinned. "I just might."

"Anyway—" he paused to shift since his knees were getting sore "—I think we should get started right away."

Pilar glanced at him sheepishly before hiding her face behind her free hand.

It took a few seconds for him to realize what he'd just suggested right there in church. He chuckled. "Well, that, too. After the wedding. But that's not what I was talking about.

"I think we should get married soon, so we can become adoptive parents. There are a lot of older and special-needs children waiting for good homes, and I think our home would be a great place for a few of them."

She glanced up at him, a smile pulling on her lips. "Our home. Aren't you getting a little ahead of yourself? We're not even engaged yet."

"Well, let's fix that because my knees are killing me." He chuckled, but when she looked at him and smiled, his breath hitched. "Pilar, will you be my wife? Will you marry me?"

"Yes! Yes, I'll marry you."

Zach moved to sit beside her and drew her into his arms. The kiss they shared lasted but a moment, but it seemed etched in time as they sealed the promise of their hearts at the altar.

Pilar was still smiling when he pulled away, though tears escaped from the corners of her eyes. She brushed them away with the back of her hand.

"I never believed this would happen."

"What, that I would propose to you like a cheapskate and not even have a ring yet?"

She laughed. "No, I wouldn't even have predicted something that awful."

Though she'd played along with his joke, Zach didn't want to make light of the moment. "I never would have predicted this. I thought love was only for other people—the ones who always win at cakewalks and always have prize-patrol vans hunting them down."

"But God had a plan all along."

"He does tend to do that. But one person around here seemed to know what it was."

She cocked her head to the side. "Who's that?"

He shrugged, considering. "Or maybe two. Naomi's a smart lady herself, but your mother definitely knew. Remember? She called me *novio*. Bridegroom."

Her eyes went wide. "You knew?" she shrieked. "If I'd have known that then, I would have died from embarrassment right there on the spot."

"Well, good thing you didn't realize it then." He lifted her hand to his lips and then pressed its softness against his cheek. "High school Spanish. I knew it would come in handy someday."

He met her gaze again, and Pilar stared back at him with such love shining in her eyes that his laughter died on his lips. One day, he hoped to be the man she clearly saw when she looked at him. He wanted to become that man for her.

An emotion he didn't recognize expanded in his heart. Perhaps hope? Why God had chosen to bless him with someone as wonderful as Pilar, he would never know. All he could do was accept the gift and be very grateful.

## Chapter Sixteen

Eli Cavanaugh stared at himself in the men's room mirror on the last Saturday in September, retying his bow tie for the third time. Still, it listed to the right, and one loop remained larger than the other.

"Whoever invented these things probably did it as a torture device for men on their wedding day," he grumbled.

Zach elbowed him and laughed as he tied his own bow tie in front of the next sink. He had to admit as he glanced into the mirror that, other than the ridiculous ties that both Rachel and Pilar had insisted they wear, the two of them looked downright wedding worthy in their matching black tuxedos.

"Do you have an easier time buttoning up a lab coat, Doc? Hey, I wouldn't complain too much. Think of the contortions our brides are doing across the hall to fasten those buttons and bustles and all that other frou-frou stuff they're putting on."

Eli nodded hard enough to rustle his dark blond hair. "And we'll be the luckiest men for all their efforts. The two most beautiful and intelligent and amazing brides around, and they've agreed to be bound in holy matrimony with this sorry pair."

"Fortunately for us, the pickings were slim in Chestnut Grove." Zach patted him on the back good-naturedly.

"You've got that right."

Zach became serious as he turned to his friend. "I wanted to thank you and Rachel again for letting us weasel in on your wedding at the last minute. That was really great of you guys."

Eli shook his head. "No weaseling at all. It was an invitation. Rachel already had a plan in mind when we left the hospital the day Ashley was there. You and Pilar hadn't even figured out that you belonged together, and she was already thinking who she needed to call to send out last-minute changes to the invitations, making it a double wedding."

"Did everyone know but us?"

Eli only grinned into the mirror.

"Anyway, I'm amazed that Rachel would want to share her day. The wedding day is so important to some women."

"Her friends are important to my soon-to-be wife."

"You are blessed, buddy." Zach paused, a grin forming on his face. "We both are."

Eli turned to him and cocked his head. "What's this I hear about a Jamaican honeymoon?"

Zach shrugged and grinned. "A little wedding present from my folks. They wanted to pamper the woman who smartened me up enough to finally work on our problems."

He didn't have to explain about his scars now because Eli already knew. The four of them had shared a lot of time and stories while they frantically turned a wedding for two into a ceremony for four in two weeks. It was a relief no longer having to keep his secret inside.

"Are they here today?"

"Mom said she'd be here with bells on, and Dad said he'd be the one with a flower between his teeth."

Eli raised an eyebrow. "All-righty then. I'm sure I'll be able to pick them out."

"I just wish Jasmine could be here. You would have liked her."

He patted Zach on the shoulder. "If she was anything like you, I'm sure I would."

Zach swallowed, pushing the heavy emotion aside. "I bet you're looking forward to Cape Cod."

Eli let out a sigh. "Quiet and sand and rest. Just me and the woman I love without taking my pager or being on call. It's the best thing I can think of this side of Heaven."

A knock had them both turning back toward the door.

"Is everyone decent in there?" Naomi called through the wood. "Hope so, because I'm coming in."

She waited, though, for one of the men to pull open the door, and the redhead bustled through, carrying a handled basket filled with small bottles and tubes. In one of her fanciest Sunday dresses and her usual pearls, Naomi had noted the special occasion by adding fancy baubles at her ears.

"Don't you look lovely today," Zach said, pretending that every day he saw a woman—and particularly the minister's wife—in the men's room.

"Knock it off, Zach. Save your flattery for your brides." But she grinned anyway and gave them both hugs. "Now remember this." She gave each of them a firm look. "We wives still like to hear how pretty we are, even after the wedding. And especially after the babies come."

Eli chuckled. "Can we at least eat some wedding cake first before we think about babies?"

Naomi patted her index finger on her lips and rolled her eyes heavenward as if considering, and then glanced back at them. "Okay, but only a small piece." She grinned and then pinned them with her pointed index finger. "And I'd better not see either of you smashing it in your brides' faces and getting their veils all sticky."

Zach answered for them both. "We'll be on our best behavior. We promise."

"Good. Now what do we have left to do here?" She studied them critically and then stepped forward. "Two bow ties coming up."

Marching up to Eli first, she signaled for him to bend his well-over-six-foot frame. "You didn't think I was coming up there, did you?"

She made quick work of Eli's tie and moved on to

Zach's. When she was done, Zach glanced into the mirror, impressed. "Hey, you're pretty good at that."

"Better than my cooking?" She lifted an eyebrow.

He shook his head. "Oh, no...uh—"

"I'm going to let you off the hook on that one, Zach. It's my wedding gift to you." She glanced at Eli. "To you, too."

"Now do you need anything else?" She lifted her basket. "I have travel toothbrushes, hair gel, shaving cream and a razor, safety pins, a pair of men's black socks, tuxedo button covers, cuff links..."

"What is all that stuff?" Eli asked.

"The groom's survival kit. Everyone always worries about the bride, so she's surrounded by bridesmaids and relatives. The groom has to send all of his ushers out to work, so he's left there alone, waiting and sweating. It's my job to make sure the groom gets to the altar in one piece and without his shirttails hanging out."

"Well, we're all tucked." Eli even lifted his jacket to pass inspection.

"Good then, because there are a lot of people waiting out there to see you two."

"This is it." Rachel gripped Pilar's lace-covered arms and gave her a squeeze, careful not to muss either of their hairdos, veils or gowns. "We made it happen."

"We sure did." Pilar squeezed back, taking the same care. "I still can't believe it."

"This day is just perfect," Rachel sighed.

Pilar couldn't help smiling at her friend. "You make a beautiful bride."

Instead of the elaborate updo that so many brides selected, Rachel wore her hair long and flowing with a dusting of spiral curls visible under her long veil. Loving Eli had transformed Rachel in so many ways beyond the change in both of their hearts when they returned to God. She'd never looked more beautiful or more relaxed than she did at this moment when jitters would have been expected.

"Look who's talking." Rachel grinned. "Love looks good on you, girlfriend."

Their circle widened as the four bridesmaids gathered both of them in a loose hug of tulle, lace, white silk and rose-colored satin. Pilar smiled at their bridesmaids— each one first invited by Rachel but all she would have chosen herself. Meg stood between Kelly and Anne, and Dinah Fraser, her sweet auburn-haired friend who had vivid blue eyes just like her mother, stood on Anne's other side. Of course, Pilar also would have included Rachel, but this idea was even better than that.

"I'm so happy for you both," Anne said as she gave each of her friends a squeeze.

Pilar could see that she really meant it, too, even though her eyes were shining. She loved Anne even more for her ability to be genuinely happy when she had to be feeling lonely with all of her close friends marrying. She would have to remember to have lunches more frequently with Anne after Pilar and Zach returned from their honeymoon.

Up the aisle, the groomsmen were already in place. Again, they were the friends she would have selected herself if she'd been the one planning the wedding from the start: Jonah Fraser, Jared Kierney and Eli's brother, Ben. Even Ramon stood at the altar, looking suave in his tux and making the young girls swoon. Her brother caught her eye and winked. Maybe he was ready to forgive her for marrying a police officer now that Zach had talked with him and promised to meet with leaders of the Hispanic community to promote better police relations.

Scanning the rest of the packed sanctuary, she was surprised not to find Zach at all. Anxiety formed in the pit of her stomach, but she tried to ignore it. Of course, he would be there. He'd promised, and she'd believed him. Come to think of it, the other groom wasn't anywhere to be found, either.

She turned to see if Rachel could clear up the mystery, but a rustling at her feet caught her attention. Meg and Jared's twins, Luke and Chance, had already turned one of the ring bearers' pillows into a pretend football and were trying to punt it. Pilar grinned as Meg took her sons in hand and quietly restored order to their tiny tuxedos.

Olivia Cavanaugh pressed by them, looking far older than her seven years in her frilly flower girl dress. She was carefully holding the hand of Rachel's baby sister, Gracie, who was all dolled up in ruffles and lace.

"Miss Rachel—I mean *Aunt* Rachel, I see Daddy up there, but I don't see Uncle Eli."

Rachel kissed Olivia on top of her light brown hair and then bent to nuzzle Gracie's curls. "Don't you worry. Everything's going to be just fine. You go ahead down the aisle, just like we showed you."

At least someone wasn't worried. Pilar sure was, and she didn't like herself for it.

"Okay, boys, it's your turn," Meg told her sons. "Walk very slowly and then go to Daddy, okay?"

Though they'd practiced the boys' entrance three times the night before and they'd never gotten it right, the twins made a flawless entrance. As the bridesmaids entered next, Pilar suddenly wished there were more of them so they could stall a little longer.

Where were the grooms?

She flashed a panicked look back to Rachel and her father, Charles, but her friend only mouthed, "Don't worry." How could she not worry when they were at a double wedding ceremony and short two grooms?

But as soon as the organ music changed in a signal for the crowd to rise for the brides, the door beside the choir loft popped open, and out came two of the most handsome grooms she'd ever seen. As Zach stared at her in awe, she immediately forgave him for the moments of panic before.

"Are you ready, *Princesa?*" Salvador Estes brushed aside a tear as he held out his arm.

Pilar smiled up at him and slipped her arm through

his. Princess. Her father would always see her that way though she was all grown up. *"Sí, Papi."*

Soon she was walking down the aisle to her groom and her future. She could barely comprehend Reverend Fraser's lovely words as Zach took her hand and stared into her eyes. She never wanted to look away.

*Thank You, Lord, for Zach and for Your perfect plan for our lives. I can't wait to live every minute of it.*

At the sound of someone clearing his throat, she jerked her head to look at the minister.

"That was for you, too, Pilar," Rachel said in a loud whisper that was caught on Reverend Fraser's microphone.

She felt her face go hot as the crowd chuckled. Zach only smiled when she turned back to him. Somehow they made it through the rest of their vows, and before she knew it, Zach was pulling her into his arms for their first kiss as husband and wife.

"I'd like to present to you for the first time Eli Cavanaugh and Rachel Noble-Cavanaugh and Zach and Pilar Fletcher," Reverend Fraser announced, already having checked their preferences.

The crowd erupted in cheers as the four of them and their entourage returned up the center aisle. Before any of the guests had been ushered out into the vestibule, Zach wrapped his arms around Pilar and kissed her until she was breathless.

"Hey, you two, quit steaming up the church windows," Eli called out, but he only turned and kissed his own bride.

Rachel chuckled as she pressed her forehead to Eli's. "Okay, tell me, dear, where you two were until we came down the aisle. Pilar, here, thought you were standing us up at the altar."

Eli shrugged. "We just wanted you two to see us during our wedding at the same time that we first saw you. It was pretty effective, wasn't it?"

She nodded. "Very effective."

But Zach turned and stared down at his bride. "You weren't really worried, were you? You had to know I would be there."

Pilar smiled up at him. "I knew."

He grinned. "Good, because I was out getting your wedding present ready."

"Present?"

He pointed to the double glass doors leading to the outside. There on the church's porch was a picnic basket. Pilar glanced up at her husband and grinned before draping her train over her arm and heading out the door.

"It doesn't have the same precious cargo as the other one." Zach lifted the intricately weaved basket and opened it for her to see. Inside this one was a checkered blanket with matching napkins and picnic-style cutlery. "But I figured we could make some of our own memories to go inside it."

"Thank you. Thank you." Pilar leaned forward and kissed her husband right over the top of the basket. He seemed startled but delighted that she'd enjoyed his gift.

Hearing laughter behind them, Pilar and Zach turned

to see Eli and Rachel playing peekaboo with Gracie, the child both of them adored.

"I bet we won't be the only ones with a house full of kids," Zach whispered in her ear.

Guests started pouring out from the sanctuary then, so they gathered for the receiving line. Pilar accepted the hugs, kisses and well-wishes with enthusiasm while sneaking occasional peeks at her new husband. Each time she glanced at him, he was looking back.

The guest list was like a who's who among Chestnut Grove's elite as well as its regular folk, thanks to Eli and Rachel's wide list of friends. Pilar did her best to make small talk with Mayor Morrow and his wife but it was much easier to laugh with their charming black-haired youth minister, Caleb Williams. As he kissed her cheek, she wondered why someone hadn't already snapped up the handsome man of God.

When Ashley Harcourt came through the line, proudly carrying Gabriel, both Zach and Pilar hugged her at once. Pilar dropped a kiss on the baby's head, pleased he was going to get to grow up in a family that loved him.

"And these are your parents," Pilar said before Zach had the chance to introduce Will and Carol Fletcher. She would have known them anywhere. Will looked like a silver-haired version of his son, and Carol, who had almost-black hair with barely a hint of gray, looked out at her with eyes so similar to the ones Zach constantly focused on her.

"Thank you" was all Carol said before drawing Pilar into her embrace. She knew immediately she would love her new mother-in-law.

"I can't believe it. You're here," Rachel exclaimed as she threw her arms around a strikingly handsome man with black hair and huge hazel eyes.

She turned to them. "Eli, Zach and Pilar, I'd like you to meet my favorite cousin, Andrew Noble."

"It's a pleasure," Andrew said as he shook their hands.

Rachel's cousin barely had time to offer his congratulations before she pulled him back over. "Aunt Clara said you were, and I quote, 'unavailable' when I sent the invitation. Are you taking more *assignments* that you won't tell me anything about?"

Andrew smiled. "We'll talk more at the reception."

Rachel grinned back at him. "And you still won't tell me anything."

When the last of the guests had come through the line and had headed into the church hall for the dinner reception, Zach reached over and took Pilar's hand.

"I love my gift," she told him. "It's perfect." And so was their romance that had begun with a baby on the doorstep and had led them to the altar.

He kissed her forehead. "You're perfect."

She shook her head. "Not at all. You just love me."

"You, Mrs. Fletcher, are right about that."

# *Epilogue*

Anne was already waiting at their usual table and holding a menu she wouldn't order from when Meg arrived for Sunday brunch at the Starlight Diner. Meg couldn't get over how small and alone her friend looked in that huge booth all by herself.

That wasn't fair, she reminded herself, as she made her way back to Anne. Just because she was happily married didn't mean she needed to push that status on everyone she knew.

Lowering her menu, Anne stood to give her friend a hug. "You're here!"

"Barely. Are you as exhausted as I am?"

Anne nodded and folded her hands by her head as though she could sleep right there at the table. Then she opened her eyes. "Wait. You forgot to recognize our buddy James."

"Oops." Meg turned and gave an exaggerated salute

to the photo of fallen actor James Dean. It was part of their tradition, and she had the feeling tradition was going to be important to Anne for a while, now that three out of the four friends were married.

"Where do you think they are now?"

Meg shrugged. "Zach and Pilar are probably getting the worst sunburn of their lives in Jamaica, and Eli and Rachel are probably sitting around with their teeth chattering and wishing they'd brought parkas and mittens to Cape Cod."

Anne chuckled. "Some romantic you are. I feel sorry for Jared."

Meg laughed with her. "Okay, Pilar and Zach are sitting on the beach, wiggling their toes in the sand and holding hands. Rachel and Eli are snuggled up by a crackling fire sharing their hopes and dreams for the future."

"That's better. I guess we can keep you."

"You'd better."

Miranda Jones approached them then, carrying two glasses of water when she could easily have balanced four or more.

"Afternoon, ladies." She looked back and forth between them. "Small crowd today."

Meg smiled. "Intimate."

"Yes, intimate." The waitress glanced around the room as if suddenly uncomfortable before returning her attention to the notebook in her apron. "May I take your order?"

Meg went with tea and toast, sorry she'd eaten so much rich food at the reception the night before.

"I'll have a double bacon cheeseburger and fries," Anne chimed, though the waitress had probably already written it down and Isaac Tubman was probably already in the kitchen flipping the burger on the grill.

As Miranda started to walk away, she turned back. "How was the wedding?"

"Beautiful and long," Anne told her. "I have the blisters on my feet to prove it."

"I wish I could have made it, but I had to work."

Meg nodded and wished the single mom had found a way to get the night off. She didn't seem to have much of a social life outside the diner. "I'm sure Rachel and Pilar missed you. They probably missed Sandra, too. Have you heard anything from her? How's her chemo going?"

Miranda smiled. "She's hanging in there. She's going to try to come back to work next week, so I'm sure she'll be serving your table again, like usual."

Funny, the waitress's voice sounded wistful. Maybe she'd enjoyed getting to be the one to serve them in Sandra's absence. Had she hoped they would become closer friends, especially since they were all about the same age? The truth was she didn't know an awful lot about Miranda Jones, but she decided she wouldn't keep it that way.

When Miranda shuffled to the kitchen, Meg turned back to Anne, who was frowning. "Everything has changed, hasn't it?"

She shook her head. "No. Not really."

But Anne crossed her arms and leaned back into the seat. "Everyone's going to have more family obligations. Getting away for brunch isn't going to be as easy."

Meg's heart went out to her friend, who was feeling unsure of herself. She'd always wished she could do or say something to convince Anne that she was beautiful inside and out, that the orthopedic shoes didn't matter. Maybe if she believed it, she would stop trying to disappear into the crowd by wearing plain clothes and no makeup.

"Anne." She reached over and touched her friend's hand. "Jared and I have the twins. I still almost never miss brunch. It's important to me. I know it's just as important to Pilar and Rachel."

She shrugged. "Maybe you're right."

"Of course I'm right. Would there ever be a question about that?"

After that, brunch went smoothly, with Meg describing some of Luke and Chance's antics and Anne chatting about the positive comments she'd been getting on Jared's newspaper series.

"I just wish Zach could figure out who broke into the office and set the fire so we could get past all this negativity," Anne said over her last French fry.

Meg nodded, figuring if Anne could ignore the significance of those tampered birth records, so could she for now. Until the many questions involving those records were answered, she doubted things would ever return to normal at the adoption agency.

When they were finished eating and Meg could no longer fight off her yawns, they decided to head home.

She gave Anne a quick hug. "For one more Sunday, you'll have to put up with just me again, but then we'll all be back together again."

Anne nodded, her worried expression softening. "You'll be in after church, right?"

"Right after." Meg was so tempted to invite Anne to church again that she had to bite her tongue to stop herself. She'd tried a few times since she and Jared had starting attending together, but Anne always had other plans. Pushing her wasn't going to help. She would come to God when she was ready.

"I'll save the booth."

"I'll see you then if not before."

With a wave, Meg headed out the restaurant door, but her friend hung behind. She wanted to turn around and go back, but she never wanted her friend to suspect that she might feel sorry for her. She loved her; that was all.

As she climbed into her car, Meg glanced one more time at the nearly empty diner. Coming out the front door, Anne smiled at her and waved. Meg smiled back, feeling much more confident about her friend. She felt certain God had something special in store for dear sweet Anne. He certainly hadn't let any of them down yet.

Meg yawned again and pressed her hand to her tummy. The tea and toast hadn't done the trick. She still

felt queasy. As she drove, she did some mental calcula-
tions. The answer to her math made her smile. Maybe
a trip to the drugstore was in order. She just might have
some great news for Jared and the boys.

* * * * *

Dear Reader,

I hope you enjoyed this visit with the people of Chestnut Grove, Virginia, and Pilar and Zach's journey to love as much as I enjoyed writing it. Pilar's character spoke to my heart because she questions God's plan for her life, as we all do sometimes. Only, in Pilar's case, she's questioning it for the very first time. Zach, on the other hand, reminds me of myself and my own Christian walk, as he searches endlessly for answers instead of simply trusting. The arrival of little Gabriel on the doorstep helps the two of them find their way to each other and to a closer relationship with God.

We never know God's purpose, only that it is perfect and that in time His answers will be revealed. "Trust in the Lord with all your heart and lean not on your own understanding"—Proverbs 3:5.

I always enjoy hearing from readers. Please feel free to write to me at P.O. Box 2251, Farmington Hills, MI 48333-2251 or contact me through the following Web sites: www.SteepleHill.com or www.loveinspiredauthors.com.

May God grant you joy along the journey,

Dana Corbit

*Anne finds herself made over by the teens
from the youth center as part of
THE CINDERELLA PLAN,
coming only to Love Inspired in October 2005.
For a sneak preview, please turn the page.*

Caleb swung around and faced her. "The youth committee working on the fund-raiser decided this year to charge a flat fee for the event and have all the adults dress up in costumes representing their favorite fairy-tale characters. There'll be an article in the newspaper tomorrow."

"I dressed in a costume for the article," Gina said, shoving her chair toward the table. "We're even going to provide costumes for people who need them. Nikki's aunt in Richmond owns a party store with lots of costumes she's going to let us have for the day."

That didn't seem too bad. Anne relaxed her death hold on the knob.

Dressed all in black, Nikki lifted her head. "Yeah, there's even gonna be prizes—for the best couple costumes, the funniest one and the scariest one. The kids are gonna be the judges."

"What made you decide to do costumes this year?" Anne released her grip on the knob and moved forward.

"Adults don't play enough. We wanted to turn the tables around and run the booths, but we aren't charging for each activity like we have in the past. Fun is the theme for the night." Gina gathered up the envelopes they had been stuffing and placed them into a box.

"It sounds like you've got things under control. But if you need any help, I'll be glad to." Anne took the box from Gina.

"That's great. We could use your help. Time's running out."

Anne noticed the surprised expression on Caleb's face and wondered about it, but before she could ask him, Gina continued, "This weekend we're gonna make flyers at the center, then put them up all over town to remind everyone about the annual event one last time."

"I'll be there. What time?"

"Early. Eight."

Anne smiled. For someone who usually got up at five every morning, eight wasn't early. "Eight it is."

"Let's go, kids. We need to meet with the rest of the committee at the center in fifteen minutes. Reverend Fraser and his wife will be waiting for us." Caleb stood to the side as the three teenage girls hurried out of the open door and down the hall.

"They seem eager about the carnival. That's great to see." Anne again found herself alone with Caleb and tension, held at bay while the room was full with three teenagers, came rushing back.

"Yeah, I'm letting the kids have a bigger role in the carnival this year. Gina came to me and asked. Since the fund-raiser is all about them, it seemed a logical decision at the time, but the carnival is only ten days away."

"And there's still so much to do?"

He nodded. "Coming up with what they wanted to do took longer than I had planned, or I would have started this back at the beginning of summer rather than the end."

"It's an annual event. The important thing about the fall carnival isn't what you do, but that the proceeds go for the church youth center and the kids who use it. Everyone knows about the carnival and has probably already made plans to attend. It's always been the second weekend in October. I can help with more than the flyers if you need me to."

"Could you? Gina, Tiffany and Nikki really respond to you. This year the committee agreed that this would be a children's production with minimal oversight from us adults. But if Gina has invited you to help with the flyers, maybe you could also help with the decorating of the hall. You were the first adult outside the committee she has asked to help with the preparations."

"Then I'll see if I can wrangle an invite from her when I'm helping them on Saturday."

Relief erased the tension in his expression. "Thank you. You're a lifesaver. I haven't been sleeping like I should, worrying about this fund-raiser."

The urge to comfort him inundated her. She balled her hands at her sides to keep from touching his arm, to assure him everything would work out. "It's good to see them so involved in something that directly affects them. The youth center is all about them. They will be the ones using the new rec equipment you'll purchase with the money raised."

"I know, and I really do think it's a terrific idea that they're so involved with the carnival, but I keep telling Gina that's what I get paid the big bucks for—to worry."

"So much of what has to be done is last-minute things. It'll all come together."

"If not, I guess I could always stand on the corner with a tin cup in whatever costume the kids pick out for me to wear and beg for the money."

Anne chuckled. She loved the way Caleb could laugh at himself. His air of confidence drew her to him. She wished she felt that way about herself. "Mmm." She tapped her finger against her chin. "There are all kinds of possibilities for your costume. There's the Papa Bear from *Goldilocks and the Three Bears*. Then there's the Big Bad Wolf from *Little Red Riding Hood*. Either one would be interesting to see."

"Yeah, I'm afraid it might be. I'm just worried about wearing tights." Grinning, he headed into the hall and started for the front door.

Anne walked with him to the entrance, then watched him make his way to his white Suburban. She waved goodbye to him and the girls, hoping none of the longing she felt deep inside revealed itself. Even though she wasn't involved at the church where he was a youth minister, she did volunteer some of her time at the youth center connected to the Chestnut Grove Community Church. She'd toyed with the idea of going to the church on Sunday, but she'd never attended services while growing up, except when she was a young girl and had gone to visit Grandma Rose. Caleb made her wonder what she was missing. Sighing, Anne turned away from the door and walked back toward her office, where she could disappear into her quiet refuge and pour through those old ledgers.

## Love Inspired
# SUSPENSE
### RIVETING INSPIRATIONAL ROMANCE

Coming in October...

# S T O R M
# C L O U D S
## by Cheryl Wolverton

An urgent call from her brother, a former secret service agent whom Angelina Harding hadn't seen in years, brought her thousands of miles to Australia. Only to find him gone. And it was only with the help of his friend David Lemming that Angelina had a hope of finding him.

Steeple Hill®

*Available at your favorite retail outlet.*
*Only from Steeple Hill Books!*

# Take 2 inspirational love stories FREE!

## PLUS get a FREE surprise gift!

### Mail to Steeple Hill Reader Service™

**In U.S.**
3010 Walden Ave.
P.O. Box 1867
Buffalo, NY 14240-1867

**In Canada**
P.O. Box 609
Fort Erie, Ontario
L2A 5X3

**YES!** Please send me 2 free Love Inspired® novels and my free surprise gift. After receiving them, if I don't wish to receive anymore, I can return the shipping statement marked cancel. If I don't cancel, I will receive 4 brand-new novels every month, before they're available in stores! Bill me at the low price of $4.24 each in the U.S. and $4.74 each in Canada, plus 25¢ shipping and handling and applicable sales tax, if any*. That's the complete price and a savings of over 10% off the cover prices—quite a bargain! I understand that accepting the books and gift places me under no obligation ever to buy any books. I can always return a shipment and cancel at any time. Even if I never buy another book from Steeple Hill, the 2 free books and the surprise gift are mine to keep forever.

113 IDN DZ9M
313 IDN DZ9N

| | | |
|---|---|---|
| Name | (PLEASE PRINT) | |
| Address | Apt. No. | |
| City | State/Prov. | Zip/Postal Code |

**Not valid to current Love Inspired® subscribers.**

*Want to try two free books from another series?*
**Call 1-800-873-8635 or visit www.morefreebooks.com.**